"Ted? What on earth is the problem?" Jillian asked.

He wanted to kick himself for having to upset her. He loved this woman so much. He had loved her almost from the first moment he'd seen her.

There was only one way to go, Ted realized, and he took it, stating bluntly, "I've been transferred to San Francisco, effective tomorrow morning. For two years."

Jillian pulled free of his hands and seemed to stumble almost blindly toward the reclining chair, collapsing into it, still staring at him and slowly shaking her head. "Transferred? To *San Francisco*? Two *years*?"

She put a hand to her mouth, her voice muffled as she said, "*Tomorrow?* This is a joke, isn't it? I mean, we're still on our honeymoon!"

Dear Reader,

Whether it's a vacation fling in some far-off land, or falling for the guy next door, there's something irresistible about summer romance. This month, we have an irresistible lineup for you, ranging from sunny to sizzling.

We continue our FABULOUS FATHERS series with *Accidental Dad* by Anne Peters. Gerald Marsden is not interested in being tied down! But once he finds himself the temporary father of a lonely boy, *and* the temporary husband of his lovely landlady, Gerald wonders if he might not actually enjoy a permanent role as "family man."

Marie Ferrarella, one of your favorite authors, brings us a heroine who's determined to settle down—but not with a man who's always rushing off to another archaeological site! However, when Max's latest find shows up *In Her Own Backyard,* Rikki makes some delightful discoveries of her own....

The popular Phyllis Halldorson returns to Silhouette Romance for a special story about reunited lovers who must learn to trust again, in *More Than You Know*. Kasey Michaels brings her bright and humorous style to a story of love at long distance in the enchanting *Marriage in a Suitcase*.

Rounding out July are two stories that simmer with passion and deception—*The Man Behind the Magic* by Kristina Logan and *Almost Innocent* by Kate Bradley.

In the months to come, look for more titles by your favorite authors—including Diana Palmer, Elizabeth August, Suzanne Carey, Carla Cassidy and many, many more!

Happy reading!

Anne Canadeo
Senior Editor

MARRIAGE IN A SUITCASE
Kasey Michaels

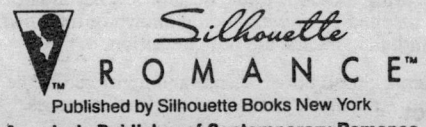
Published by Silhouette Books New York
America's Publisher of Contemporary Romance

If you purchased this book without a cover you should be aware that this book is stolen property. It was reported as "unsold and destroyed" to the publisher, and neither the author nor the publisher has received any payment for this "stripped book."

To my readers—thank you so much!

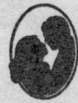

SILHOUETTE BOOKS
300 East 42nd St., New York, N.Y. 10017

MARRIAGE IN A SUITCASE

Copyright © 1993 by Kasey Michaels

All rights reserved. Except for use in any review, the reproduction or utilization of this work in whole or in part in any form by any electronic, mechanical or other means, now known or hereafter invented, including xerography, photocopying and recording, or in any information storage or retrieval system, is forbidden without the permission of the publisher, Silhouette Books, 300 E. 42nd St., New York, N.Y. 10017

ISBN: 0-373-08949-X

First Silhouette Books printing July 1993

All the characters in this book have no existence outside the imagination of the author and have no relation whatsoever to anyone bearing the same name or names. They are not even distantly inspired by any individual known or unknown to the author, and all incidents are pure invention.

®: Trademark used under license and registered in the United States Patent and Trademark Office and in other countries.

Printed in the U.S.A.

Books by Kasey Michaels

Silhouette Romance

Maggie's Miscellany #331
Compliments of the Groom #542
Popcorn and Kisses #572
To Marry at Christmas #616
His Chariot Awaits #701
Romeo in the Rain #743
Lion on the Prowl #808
Sydney's Folly #834
Prenuptial Agreement #898
Uncle Daddy #916
Marriage in a Suitcase #949

Silhouette Books

Spring Fancy 1993
"Simon Says..."

KASEY MICHAELS,

the author of more than two dozen books, divides her creative time between writing contemporary romance and Regency novels. Married and the mother of four, Kasey's writing has garnered the Romance Writers of America Golden Medallion Award and the *Romantic Times* Best Regency Trophy.

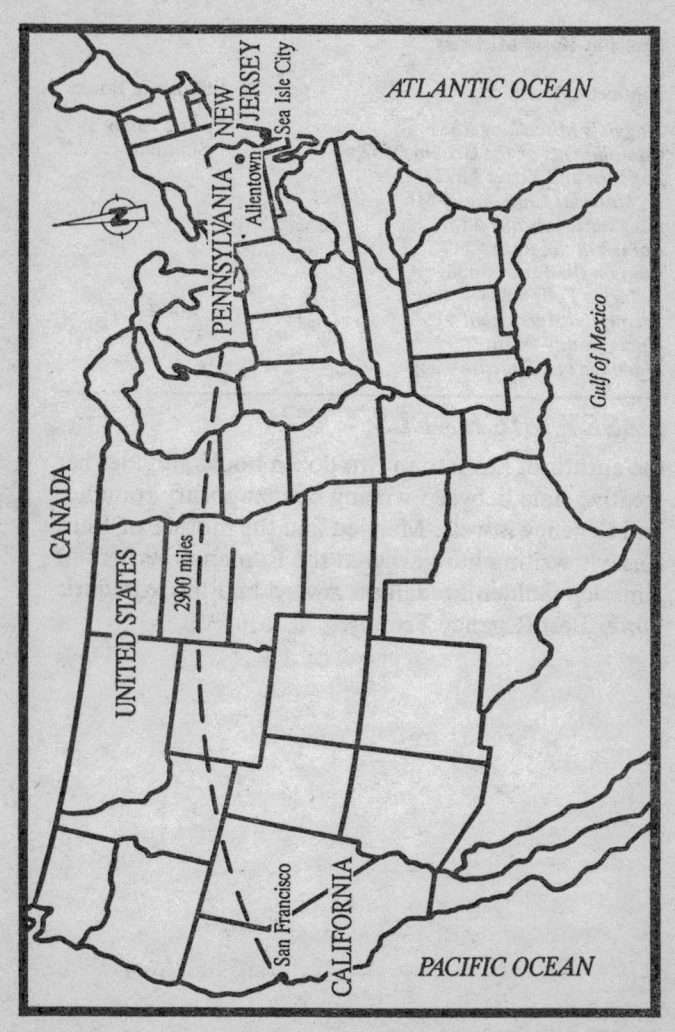

Prologue

It was a beautiful June day.

Jillian Hackett reclined on a slatted wooden bench beside the sun-drenched tennis court, taking sips of ice-cold soda, and watched in affectionate amusement as Ted, her husband of three whole days, systematically went about annihilating his latest opponent, a thirty-something insurance agent from Tennessee.

Jillian had played two sets against Ted earlier this afternoon, fighting him all the way, daring him to allow her to win simply because she was his bride and this was their honeymoon.

But she should have known better than to worry that Ted would have let her beat him just to be "nice." He had battled her for every point, and he had won each set—6-3, 6-2.

Ted didn't know the meaning of the word *lose*. It simply wasn't a part of his vocabulary.

Nor did it play a very large part in her own philosophy of life, Jillian reflected with a self-deprecating sigh, which was probably how they had first become attracted to each other that memorable day four months earlier on a handball court at the health club to which they both belonged.

Jillian had been a new member at the time and worked out often. There was something about physical exercise that, to her, had become almost addictive. She knew herself to be fiercely competitive, and she believed her drive to win to be a virtue and not a failing.

And so, on that fateful, wonderful day—after sending her latest handball opponent to the showers a defeated woman—Jillian had only grinned in anticipation when the door to the handball court had opened. A moment later Ted Hackett, whom she had seen once or twice at the club, had stuck his darkly handsome face in and said, "Killed off another easy mark, I see. But are you ready for a *real* contest?"

Jillian smiled again now, remembering how they had battled that day, neither one giving the other quarter. An hour later, having lost the rubber game on the very last point, she had been bent over, her hands on her knees, her copper-colored ponytail falling forward over her forehead, trying desperately to remember how to breathe, when Ted had announced, "It's almost dinnertime. Loser buys—or did I somehow forget to mention that?"

"Yes, as a matter of fact, I believe you did," she had replied, rather stung to think he might be taking advantage of her. Did he have to rub in his victory? Wasn't it enough that he stood a good eight inches higher than her five-foot-six-inch frame and had wide shoulders that would look positively ludicrous if he ever tried to stuff them into her compact car?

But when she had lifted her head and looked into his laughing blue eyes, she realized that she might have overreacted. He was just being friendly. "Okay, loser buys. I'll meet you in the lounge in about twenty minutes. Hope you like fast food—I'm on a budget."

She had showered and dressed in record time, before slipping into the navy cotton skirt and flowered blouse she'd worn to her substitute teacher's job earlier.

After hurriedly inspecting her appearance in a full-length mirror, she strolled with studied nonchalance to the lounge, sure she would have beaten him there—only to see Ted leaning against the bar, already sipping a tall glass of iced tea.

He had looked wonderful. She had expected him to be dressed in casual sweats, or if he had come to the health club straight from work as she had done, in a dark business suit.

Instead, his long body was clothed in a severely styled navy blue uniform with shiny gold buttons and some sort of insignia on his lapels. A military-style hat sat next to him on the bar and a black leather weekend-size suitcase was at his feet.

As she had stepped closer she realized that Ted was dressed in the uniform of an airline pilot, the words Lombard Airways embroidered on his chest pocket just under the small brass tag bearing his name.

Jillian had been surprised and vaguely impressed. It must be true, she thought—there definitely is something very attractive about a man in uniform. Hadn't her first real boyfriend been an Eagle Scout?

She suddenly regretted her suggestion of dinner at some fast-food place and was about to ask Ted if he wanted to visit a new restaurant that had just opened on Hamilton Boulevard.

But before she could speak, Ted had set down his glass, taken her arm and announced, "Lead me to those Golden Arches, Miss Connors. If we hurry, we'll still have time to grab an early movie before I catch my red-eye flight to Tampa."

"A real take-charge kind of guy, aren't you?" Jillian asked, already moving in step with him as they headed for the flight of stairs that led to the street. "Just remember—the movie's on you!"

By the end of the evening Jillian had realized that Ted Hackett was much more than a "take-charge kind of guy." He was nice, friendly and devastatingly handsome. He was also a most interesting man—and his good-night kiss had more power to rob her of breath than an entire afternoon on the handball court.

Ted, she had learned over the next few weeks, was a flight engineer for Lombard Airways, currently working flights from the Allentown-Bethlehem-Easton International Airport to Florida. He had loved flying since his early childhood and had spent four years in the air force before coming to Pennsylvania and landing his job with Lombard.

He had taken the flight-engineering job because no other positions were open at the time, but hoped to be promoted to pilot status within three years—a personal goal that she had no reason to question.

It was difficult to question anything Ted Hackett said, because he absolutely oozed confidence as well as charm. He had been immediately interested in her own work as a semipermanent substitute second-grade teacher at a local private school, and although their dates had to be sandwiched in between his flights and her own commitments, they never seemed to run out of conversation.

In short, they were compatible—in every way. Yes, Jillian could admit to herself, there were moments when their personalities clashed, a slight problem she was sure resulted from their equally strong desires to be the best at whatever they did—teaching school, navigating a large passenger jet, playing handball or even figuring out who the murderer in a new movie was by the end of the first reel.

Yet Jillian had never felt so alive in her twenty-four years, and when Ted took her in his arms and kissed her she knew that he was the reason for her new happiness.

Ted, bless him, had also never been so happy, or at least that was what he had told her when he'd surprised her with an emerald-cut diamond on the two-month anniversary of their first date.

As Jillian's mother had moved to Spain with her new husband during Jillian's last year of college and Ted's parents were deceased, they had opted for a small wedding as soon as the school term was over for the summer, with only Jack Borden, Ted's friend from high school, and Jillian's best friend, Barbara, in attendance.

And then, with only a three-day weekend in which to celebrate before Ted took off for Tampa once more, they had come to the New Jersey seaside town of Sea Isle City, for their honeymoon.

"And if I don't soon stop reminiscing and get him off this blinking tennis court, we won't have time for a romantic, newlywed-type walk on that lovely, wide beach before we have dinner," she muttered under her breath.

Slowly rising from the bench and stretching in order to work out any muscle kinks left over from their earlier match, she called out brightly, "Hey, Mr. Super Hero—you about done?"

Ted, interrupted in his serving motion, turned and winked at her. "One more ace should wrap it up,

Slugger," he called back. He repositioned himself for the serve and delivered the ball across the net with blinding speed, leaving his amazed opponent unable to do anything more than watch it bounce just inside the line and continue on to the fence.

"You're a terrible show-off," Jillian teased a few minutes later, after Ted had shaken hands with his opponent and was walking toward the motel with her, his arm slung over her shoulders.

His teeth were very white beneath the tanned skin of his handsome face. "Only to impress you, my love," he answered, dropping a kiss on her forehead.

"Oh, be still my heart!" Jillian responded. She danced out from under his arm and headed for the sliding-glass doors that entered directly into their motel room. "Beat you to the showers!"

"Not if I can help it!" He ran after her and they raced through the room, discarding their clothing in a trail from the sliding-glass doors to the bathroom, laughing and teasing as they fought to be the first to get into the large shower stall.

Their race ended in a tie, their laughter fading under the cascade of warm water from the shower head. Their lips met in a fevered kiss, their hands reaching, stroking, embracing—and they both knew they had won in the most important game of all.

The game of love.

Chapter One

The Monday morning ride back to Allentown from Sea Isle City was a little sad, for Jillian knew that Ted would be leaving that evening for a three-day trip to Florida that included a couple of "short hops" to Louisiana, which would lengthen his stay away from her.

Not, she had told him, that it bothered her. She was a big girl now, she had explained, and quite capable of taking care of herself.

Jillian, the only child of a widowed mother, had been on her own since her senior year of college, living alone in her childhood home while commuting daily to Kutztown University, which she had attended thanks to earnings from summer jobs and some hefty student loans she was still paying off.

Jillian had become used to caring for herself, as well as caring for her mother's small brick house located on North Nineteenth Street—self-sufficient and liking it that way.

But as Ted pulled his car into the short gravel driveway that led in from the alleyway behind the house, Jillian realized for the first time that, after only three mornings of waking up with Ted lying beside her, she was not looking forward to facing tomorrow's dawn alone.

Ted had been fortunate enough to sublet his Bethlehem Township apartment to another employee of Lombard Airways and had put his furniture in storage. His clothing and an elaborate stereo system Jillian had told him seemed capable of a moon landing had been moved into her rent-free house—now *their* rent-free house—the night before the wedding.

In short, they were all set up to begin housekeeping, to begin living the rest of their lives together. So why, Jillian thought as Ted came around the front of the car to help her open the door, did she suddenly feel so sad.

"Here we are, Slugger. Home at last," Ted said using his pet name for her. *Slugger.* It wasn't exactly a romantic name, but Jillian adored it.

Let other wives have their husband's call them Sugarplum or Twinkle Toes or Little Honeybun. She'd take Slugger any day of the week. It meant that she was a fighter, a woman unafraid to step up to the "plate" of life and take her licks at bat—eager for adventure.

But mostly, Jillian acknowledged privately, she liked it because of the obvious affection evident in Ted's deep velvet-gravel voice each time he used the word as a form of endearment.

"Did you push the button that pops open the trunk?" she asked, suddenly remembering the luggage. She stood on the driveway and looked up at the house, idly wondering if they should have stopped at the local convenience store and picked up some ingredients for an omelet or sandwiches.

Ted had to leave for the airport no later than five o'clock and Jillian wasn't about to waste most of their afternoon cooking a huge dinner. This was their new home, after all, and she had every intention of properly "christening" their bedroom before he went to work.

"Did I pop the trunk? Do you really want to unpack, Slugger?" Ted questioned her incredulously, shaking his head. *"Now?"*

She smiled up into his comically scrunched up face. Obviously their minds were operating very much on the same wavelength.

"Nah," she said, launching herself into his arms, the only place, she realized happily, that she really felt at home. "At least, not if you've already got something more *interesting* in mind."

Ted didn't seem to need any further encouragement, and quickly slipping his arms beneath Jillian's shoulders and knees he lifted her high against his chest as he turned to stride long-leggedly up the brick walkway that divided the narrow yard lengthwise and led to the back door.

"Reach in my pocket and get out the key, will you, Jill? I want to carry my bride over the threshold," he said as she buried her head against his broad chest. She blushed as she wondered if any of her neighbors were looking, and then she smiled, realizing that she hoped they were.

Especially Mrs. Ottinger from the house across the alleyway, who had once told Jillian that tall, skinny, athletic girls always ended up tall, skinny old maids.

Jillian had just inserted the key into the lock—not an easy task, for Ted was nuzzling her neck as she tried to locate the keyhole—when she heard the screen door of the house attached to hers bang to a close and her name being loudly called from somewhere behind her.

"Barbara?" she questioned, lying back against Ted's shoulder and trying to twist around to see her friend and, just the other day, her maid of honor and single attendant at the wedding.

"Jill!" Barbara McAllister, a short, slightly chubby blonde with wide blue eyes—and Jillian's best friend since they were both in diapers—burst into the yard through a break in the low picket fence, waving a yellow envelope. "Thank God you're home. Something *terrible* has happened!"

"Oh, brother—here we go again," Ted grumbled into Jillian's ear, his warm breath deliciously tickling the sensitive skin of her throat. "Want to bet her washing machine broke down or something? Is everything always a life-or-death crisis for that woman?"

"Hush, you idiot—she'll hear you," Jillian warned, giggling, although she had to agree with Ted. Barbara did have a habit of redesigning any convenient molehill into a towering mountain.

But she meant well, bless her, and besides, Barbara had always been a true friend, which counted for a lot with Jillian. "You'd better put me down now, darling. This could be something important."

"Sure it could," Ted agreed, his blue eyes twinkling with mischief as he lowered Jillian to the floor of the small cement porch. "She might even have broken a nail or suffered some other life-threatening injury. But hurry up, okay, Slugger? My flight leaves at seven."

"Gosh—how I love it when you're romantic. You make it sound as if we have an appointment we have to keep."

"But we do," Ted countered, grinning at her wickedly. "A very *important* appointment—upstairs. And *alone*."

"Works for me," Jillian agreed, then patted Ted on the cheek and turned to greet Barbara, who was still waving the yellow envelope frantically, as if using it to shoo away killer bees. "Hiya, Barb. What's up? Is there a problem?"

The blonde skidded to a halt, stepped around Jillian and planted herself directly in front of Ted, all but poking the envelope in his face.

"Is there a problem? I'll say there's a problem! Thank heaven you're home at last! I can't deal with all this responsibility! This came for you yesterday morning, Ted," she explained, gasping slightly as she struggled to regain her breath. "Yesterday, Ted. On a *Sunday!*"

"Really? On a *Sunday*," Ted said, winking at Jillian. "Look at this, Slugger. It looks like a telegram, not that I can really see it. Maybe we've won ten million dollars from that contest I entered."

"Hardly." Barbara sniffed audibly. "I was outside, planting petunias—you remember, Jill. I told you I bought four flats of petunias, two for you and two for me. I picked pink and white ones this year, since you weren't around to help me decide. You see, Ted, when front yards are small, like ours are, it looks nice if they match. Jill's mother and mine started the tradition decades ago."

"And—" Jillian prompted.

"Oh, yeah, right. *And* I was outside, down on all fours in the dirt, sticking those darn petunias in the ground, when this came for you, Ted, so I volunteered to take it—although I didn't want to do it, really I didn't."

"Thanks, Barb—for the petunias, the history lesson and for taking delivery of my mail, even if you didn't want to do it."

Ted frowned, reaching for the envelope, but Barbara pulled back her hand as if she'd just had second thoughts about handing it over to him.

She turned to Jillian. "You should have told me which hotel you were staying at, Jill, so that I could have telephoned you. But how could I do that even if I did know where you were staying—and ruin your honeymoon with bad news? I mean, what sort of friend would I be if I did that? It's addressed to Ted, but maybe you'd better read it first, Jill. After all—it's a *telegram*. From *Western Union*. Somebody died."

"Died? Who died?" Jillian snatched the telegram from Barbara's grip and held it up to the sunlight, hoping to see through the envelope.

"For pity's sake, Barb, how can you know that? This hasn't even been opened." She frowned. "Besides, it's probably just a congratulatory wire from one of Ted's buddies. Isn't that right, darling?" she asked, looking up at him, wishing he'd step in and rescue her from Barbara's flight of fancy.

He smiled, showing the faint dimple in his left cheek that she had grown to love. "Oh, I don't know," he said teasingly. "It could be terrible news. What do you say we go inside and steam it open? Unless Barbara has already done that and then sealed it up again so that we could open it ourselves?" he ended, looking down at Jillian's blushing friend.

"No, no. Of course I didn't do that. I'd *never* do that," Barbara said huffily, then ended sheepishly, "although I did *think* about it, I suppose. I mean, it's been sitting in my living room since yesterday—*glowering* at me—ever since I told the delivery guy I'd give it to you and—"

"Relax, Barb, Ted's only teasing. Ted, tell Barb you're teasing," Jillian said as her husband opened the door and all three of them stepped inside the small enclosed back porch that had been converted to a laundry room and pantry.

She felt a small pang of regret that Ted hadn't been able to carry her over the threshold, but at least he had planned to do so. The thought ought to count for something, she supposed. "Why don't we go into the living room and sit down?"

Barbara followed them through the kitchen and dining room and into the living room, apologizing profusely all the way. "I suppose I should have waited until later, shouldn't I? Ted was all set to carry you over the threshold—just like in the movies—and I blew it for you. I'm sorry, Jilly, honey, honest I am. But everyone knows a telegram means bad news. Somebody died, I'm sure of it. At least, *something* terrible has happened."

"Right," Ted said, collapsing his long frame into the ancient, faintly battered tweed recliner that had belonged to Jillian's father, the chair Ted had long since claimed as his own. "Well, I don't know about the rest of you, but this suspense is damn near killing me. Slugger, why don't you open the telegram and get it over with?"

That had been Jillian's intention. She had planned to open the telegram, proudly read out the congratulatory message from one of Ted's friends, then quickly shuffle Barbara out of the house and drag her husband upstairs to the master bedroom—for their "important appointment."

But now Jillian wasn't quite so sure. What if Barbara was right? What if the telegram did contain bad news? Barbara's doom-and-gloom predictions—a trait Jillian suspected her friend had inherited from her overly cautious mother—had been known to be right before.

Okay. Not often. But *sometimes*.

"Jillian—do you want me to open it?"

She looked to Ted, who seemed so calm, so collected, so *strong*. Biting her bottom lip, she nodded mutely, crossed the room and handed it to him, then sat beside Barbara on the couch, giving her friend a nervous smile. It was nice to be married, her smile told Barbara, and it was even nicer to have someone else to lean on sometimes.

"Well, how about that," Ted said a moment later, having ripped open the envelope and pulled out the telegram. He sat forward on the chair, shaking his head as he read the long message for what had to be at least the third time. "Damn! How about that!"

And then he smiled—an obviously happy, yet oddly sad smile.

"How about *what,* gosh darn it?" Jillian hopped from her seat and raced over to him. She tried to snatch the telegram from his hand, but he moved it behind his back, out of her reach. "Ted Hackett, if you don't tell me what's in that telegram within the next five seconds I'll—I'll murder you!"

"You'll probably murder me if I do tell you, Slugger," he said, pulling her down onto his lap, then lightly kissed her cheek.

"Then it *is* bad news, after all?" Barbara sprang up from the couch and raced over to the recliner, to stand looking down at Jillian, frowning fiercely. "I don't get it. It's bad news and he's *laughing?* Geez, Jill, is he always like this? I thought you said he was brilliant."

"Slugger! You said that?" Ted inquired, giving Jillian a playful hug. "No wonder I married you. You're a woman of great perception."

"I'm a woman with a great right cross," she warned, brandishing a fist in his face. "Now tell me—tell *us,*" she amended as Barbara pointedly cleared her throat, "what does the telegram say?"

"The *telegram* doesn't say anything, Jill," he answered, although she suddenly sensed that he wasn't trying to be funny, but only attempting to draw out the inevitable—the moment when he would have to give her the information she had requested.

"The *message*," Ted continued rapidly once Jillian had playfully shaken a fist at him, "relates that I, Theodore J. Hackett—the *J* stands for Joseph, as you learned during our wedding—am now the newest first officer for Lombard Airways. With any luck, I'll be a senior pilot within two years, maybe less."

"Ted! But that's not bad news. That's absolutely *wonderful* news! It's *great* news!" Jillian exclaimed hugging his neck. "What a fantastic wedding present!" She took hold of his cheeks and planted a hard kiss on his lips, then hopped to her feet and hugged Barbara as well. "Isn't this great, Barb? Ted's going to actually be *flying* the airplanes! He's a copilot!"

She turned back to Ted. "Do they still call them copilots, darling?"

"Among other things," he answered wryly, rising to his feet, his hands shoved deep into the pockets of his khaki trousers. "I honestly hadn't expected this promotion quite so quickly. It brings a hefty pay raise with it, Slugger. We can have that house in the suburbs you and I both want a lot sooner than we'd planned—our own little dream house, with plenty of space for kids and dogs."

"Oh, Ted! That's fantastic news!" Jillian was ecstatic. She knew how much the promotion meant to Ted. As Ted had pointed out, the promotion meant a lot to *both* of them—to their future. She loved her home, and it would serve Ted and herself very well for now, but it was her mother's home, not hers. She lived there rent free, but she was responsible for utilities, taxes and upkeep, having insisted upon that arrangement in order to begin establishing her independence.

Her mother had suggested that Jillian and Ted could purchase the house from her, but they had decided against it. The house was old and none too large, and extremely costly to keep up. And, besides, it was nearly in the center of town.

They both wanted their children raised in a big, rambling house with a huge yard and plenty of other kids their own ages to play with living nearby. In their current neighborhood, the houses were small, on small property lots, and most of the residents were older, their children grown and gone. With Ted's promotion they would have a chance to fulfill their dream—and much sooner than they'd expected.

And yet something seemed wrong—or at least not quite right.

Jillian was already convinced that Ted was happy. As a matter of fact, there was nothing Ted loved more than a good celebration. But he didn't seem to be as overjoyed as he should be. Why wasn't he asking her to fetch that bottle of champagne Jack Borden had given them as a wedding present, so that they could toast his promotion?

"Ted? Darling? Is there something you aren't telling me?"

"I knew it! I knew there was something wrong!" Barbara exclaimed, tugging on Jillian's arm. "Didn't I tell you telegrams always bring bad news? Oh, I knew it, I knew it. Maybe first officers aren't allowed to be married. I'll bet that's it! I'll bet—"

"Barb," Jillian interrupted as Ted turned his back, looking out the picture window. "I love you. Honestly. But, please, do me a favor. Go home. I'll phone you later, I promise."

"Got ya," Barbara responded swiftly, looking quickly from Ted to Jillian. Then she headed out of the room without another word, only pausing at the entrance to the dining room to say, "I picked up some bread and milk, and put a hamburger casserole and a tossed salad in the refrigerator earlier, Jill. I'll just stick the casserole in the oven on my way out. It should be ready in an hour or so. Call me, okay?"

"I will—I promise. Thanks for the casserole, Barbara."

"Hey—what are friends for? Bye!"

"Ted?" Once Barbara was gone Jillian slipped her arms around his waist and laid her head against his back. "This is one of those good news, bad news sort of things, isn't it? Your promotion is obviously the good news. Now—what's the *bad* news?"

Chapter Two

Ted continued to stare through the sparkling windowpanes, watching the traffic move along North Nineteenth Street on its way either into or out of the center of town. Nineteenth Street was not exactly a major artery, but it was a fairly busy street, especially during the morning and evening rush hours, and he didn't intend to raise his kids—his and Jillian's kids—in the city.

Besides, this was Jillian's mother's house. Maybe he was too proud, too unbending, but he wanted to provide for his wife and family. Living rent free was a godsend for now, but he had been amazed the day Jillian had spread out her monthly bills for his inspection and he'd learned that she was still paying off a loan for the new roof that she'd had put on last year.

The old house was a money eater, pure and simple. The kitchen was too small and badly out of date—with no room to install a dishwasher, even if they could afford one—there was only a single bathroom, and the electrical wiring needed updating.

He and Jillian had already begun touring area sample homes on Sunday afternoons. They had even opened a special joint savings account at a nearby bank expressly to save money for short-term certificates of deposit and investments in mutual funds—the sort of thing millions of other young couples did to plan for their futures.

They needed to maintain two cars, only one of which was completely paid for, so they couldn't economize much on their transportation costs, and there was still that little matter of Jillian's outstanding student loans.

All in all, the promotion—and the resulting increase in salary—were godsends, ones he had hoped for but had not believed possible for at least another year. But there was a hitch.

There was always a hitch.

"Jill," he said now, turning around to place his hands on her upper arms, wondering how he could begin to tell her what he had to tell her. "Slugger—"

"Ted?" Jillian's green eyes were opened wide and her freckles stood out prominently on her tanned cheeks. "What on earth is the problem?"

He wanted to kick himself for having to upset her. He loved this woman so much. He had loved her almost from the first moment he'd seen her at the athletic club—her shiny copper hair scraped back in a no-nonsense ponytail, a white terry-cloth band encircling her forehead, her confident walk and bright smile exuding happiness and health and, he admitted now, *sexiness*.

There was only one way to go, Ted realized, and he took it, stating bluntly, "I've been transferred to San Francisco, effective tomorrow morning. For two years. After that, I'll be based at ABE again."

Jillian pulled free of his hands and seemed to stumble almost blindly toward the reclining chair, collapsing into it, still staring at him, and slowly shaking her head. "Transferred? To *San Francisco*? Two *years*?"

She put a hand to her mouth, her voice muffled as she said, "*Tomorrow?* This is a joke, isn't it? I mean, we're still on our honeymoon. This has *got* to be some sort of a joke!"

"It's no joke, Jillian." Ted went down on his knees in front of the chair, clasping its upholstered arms as he leaned close to his wife. "The powers that be didn't give us much notice, did they, Slugger? But I've been with Lombard long enough to know the drill. I'll be flying the San Francisco-to-Hawaii route after my initial training is completed, and then I'll be sent back here for permanent assignment unless I decide on another base. Which I won't, of course."

"No. No, of course you won't," Jillian said, her voice low and devoid of expression. Ted's heart broke for her. She had been born and raised in Allentown and had already told him that she never wanted to leave, although she would if his job demanded it.

In return, Ted had solemnly promised Jillian that once he was promoted to captain and held control over his permanent assignment he would make certain he was based at ABE, a growing international airport located in the middle of a growing Pennsylvania metropolis.

"Lombard will provide me with an apartment for the first month, if I remember correctly, and I'll start looking for a place for the two of us as soon as I can," he told her. "We won't be separated for long, Slugger. I won't allow it."

Jillian slowly leaned forward and gently cupped his cheeks between her hands, tears beginning to shine in her sad eyes.

"Ted—how can I go?" she whispered, her voice breaking. "What about my contract with Baird?" she continued as he held his breath, the truth of her words hitting home. She had signed a two-year contract with the private school as a full-time teacher. They had celebrated that contract just last week!

Ted stood, turning his back so that Jillian couldn't see how concerned he was. And how frightened. "Surely they'll let you out of it?"

"They might," she agreed, although he could tell that her heart wasn't in it. "But that wouldn't guarantee that I could get another teaching job lined up in San Francisco before the fall term. I'd have to wait until I got another job before I resigned. I don't even know if my teaching certificate would be valid in California. At the very least I'll have to take some sort of exam or something. Oh, Ted—why did this have to happen *now?*"

Ted bristled at her complaint, even though he knew he was overreacting. But, dammit, this was supposed to be a reason to celebrate! Yes, there were a few wrinkles to iron out, but did Jillian have to start raining all over his parade within five short minutes of his announcement? Couldn't she at least *pretend* to be happy for him?

He turned to face her, his arms spread wide. "What do you want me to do, Jill? Turn down the promotion?"

"No! No, of course not!" Jillian exclaimed, rising from the chair and wrapping her arms around his waist, her head pressed against his chest. "I'm happy for you, Ted, truly I am. I'm happy for *us*. It's just—it's just that it's so sudden. I've barely had time to think!"

She stood on tiptoe and kissed his cheek, although he saw the tears standing bright in her sad green eyes. "It'll work out, darling. You'll see—it will all work out just fine!"

You'll see—it will all work out just fine.

Ted remembered Jillian's hopeful words three weeks later as he climbed the single flight of stairs to his bachelor apartment at the end of another long, fruitless Saturday spent apartment hunting. Remembered them, and sighed.

San Francisco was a beautiful city, but it was also an expensive city.

Damn expensive.

As were his hour-long telephone calls to Allentown every evening.

As were his meals, either expensive microwave entrées or lunches and dinners taken on the run at local restaurants.

As were his new uniforms and his taxi rides and his purchase of the small television set he watched far into the night because he didn't want to face his single bed—his *empty* single bed.

His days were interesting and full, thank goodness, and he enjoyed his time spent in the flight simulator and the classes he took with three other newly promoted first officers, but he sure didn't feel very much like a married man.

His fellow students, all carefree bachelors, laughed when he refused to join them as they hit the local hot spots after hours, but he didn't care. He was much more interested in racing home to his telephone, his one link with Jillian. Or at least he had been. Now it wasn't so simple.

Jillian had begun her summer job, working as a playground instructor for the Allentown parks-and-recreation department, but she arrived home at five o'clock, which was only two o'clock San Francisco time. That, Ted had discovered, gave her plenty of time to think up questions to ask him before he was finally able to telephone her.

At first her questions had centered around his new job and whether or not he missed her. But lately her inquiries had become more pointed, and slightly painful.

Had he found an apartment?

Had he forwarded her latest batch of resumés to more of the local school districts in and around San Francisco?

Had he been able to arrange for some free time, so that he could fly home to Allentown to spend a weekend with her?

Had he any idea as to why her four-year-old compact car had become increasingly hard to start in the morning?

Ted slumped in the uncomfortable orange slingback canvas chair that wasn't kind to his long frame, staring at the telephone, unable to muster the energy to call Jillian and tell her that, yet again, he had failed on all counts.

Especially the four-year-old compact car "part."

He wearily rested his head against the wrought-iron frame of the chair and closed his eyes, mentally conjuring up Jillian's face as he had last seen her, smiling bravely through her tears as he had walked away from her, down the long corridor at ABE, toward the plane that would take him out of her life for only the good Lord knew how long.

They had only been married, been together, for four days. Four beautiful, glorious, never-to-be-forgotten days.

And that hadn't been enough.

Not, he acknowledged with a faint smile, that there would ever be enough time with Jillian—not if they both lived to be one hundred.

He slapped his palms against the arms of the chair and dragged himself to his feet, to stride purposefully into the small galley kitchen and retrieve a can of iced tea from the refrigerator. He could have a beer if he wanted to, for he knew he wouldn't be flying in the next twenty-four hours, but he just didn't feel in the mood for a beer.

He felt in the mood for *several* beers, but not just one, and since he never drank to excess he decided to pass on the impulse. Besides, the drunks he'd seen were usually maudlin. He didn't need any help in that particular department.

Carrying the can of iced tea in one hand, he returned to the uncomfortable canvas chair and picked up the mail that he'd brought with him from the mailbox in the downstairs entryway.

One by one he leafed through the envelopes, tossing them to the floor at his feet. *Occupant. Current resident. Occupant. To our Very Good Friend at...*

"Congratulations, Hackett, you're an official non-person," he said out loud as he was about to launch the last envelope in the general direction of the others. But then he stopped, recognizing Jillian's distinctive, bold handwriting.

He jammed the iced-tea can onto the rickety wrought-iron side table, nearly causing both to overturn, then ripped open the long envelope to reveal a greeting card.

It wasn't his birthday, was it? he asked himself, silently, as he turned the card over and looked at the whimsical drawing of a sad-faced, pigtailed, redheaded little girl dressed in a green-and-white plaid shirt and droopy jeans, her arms stretched out wide.

On the ground next to her were a baseball bat and glove, lying on a thin strip of grass. Opening the card, he read: "I miss you *this* much!"

The card was signed, "Slugger."

Ted broke speed records pushing the buttons for the area code and Jillian's telephone number, then waited impatiently through five rings before his wife answered, breathless, as if he had summoned her from a great distance—which, he mused in wry amusement as he thought about it, he had.

"Hello? Ted? Is that you?"

He settled down in the sling-back chair, suddenly refreshed, feeding on the sound of her voice. "Hiya, Slugger. Got your card."

"You did? Already? I only mailed it four days ago. Who says the mails are slow? Direct coast-to-coast-turtle service! Did you like it?"

He grinned, looking down at the redheaded cartoon drawing. "Sure did, Slugger. Looks just like you, as a matter of fact."

"Gee, thanks," Jillian answered, subtle background noises causing him to picture her subsiding slowly onto the wide bed they had inhabited only briefly the day they had returned from their honeymoon. The bed he had yet to sleep in.

"You in the bedroom?" he asked tightly, wincing as he remembered how she had looked that last afternoon, lying back on the pink flowered sheets, her coppery hair spread silkily across the pillow, her arms extended upward, inviting him to join her.

"Uh-huh. I was in the shower when you called. I quickly wrapped a towel around me and raced for the telephone. You're early tonight."

Jillian was on the bed.

Jillian was all soft and scented, straight from her shower.

Jillian's delectable body was wrapped in a fluffy towel, her long, straight legs bare, her freshly washed hair most probably hidden in another towel she'd wrapped, turban style, around her head, her creamy shoulders rising above the towel, a hint of her pulse beating softly at the base of her throat.

Enticingly at the base of her throat.

Ted wished he had opted for that can of beer.

"Ted? Are you still there?"

He blinked twice, deliberately splintering the beautiful image that had been building behind his eyes. "Yeah, dammit, I'm still here. And you're still there. So, can you tell me, Slugger—what's wrong with that picture?"

"Oh, Ted—darling," Jillian responded, her voice tinged with sadness and, he knew, a mounting frustration that probably matched his own. "As the old saying goes—is this any way to run an airline?"

He chuckled halfheartedly at her attempt at a joke. "I miss you, too, Slugger. Like hell. But, hey, it's only been three weeks—"

"—four days, twelve hours and twenty-five, no, twenty-six minutes," Jillian ended for him, and he heard her soft sigh through the telephone lines. "But, then, who's counting? Have you had any luck yet in finding an apartment, or are you destined to spend your evenings being strangled by that man-eating chair you told me about?"

The time had come to tell his wife the truth. He didn't want to, and wasn't the sort who dealt well with defeat, but he knew it was time they began being realistic about their situation.

"Slugger," he began slowly, then raced to finish, "Steve Hammond, one of the guys in my group, found a great apartment yesterday—only it's too expensive for him to carry the rent alone."

"Can we do it?"

"No. No, we can't. Oh, sure, we could—if we sold my car and didn't mind not being able to put a penny away for the next two years. And that's if you could get a job out here. I have to tell you, Slugger, it isn't looking good. Budget cutbacks, you know. Nobody's hiring teachers right now."

"Tell me about it! I got some mail today, too. I received answers on three of those resumés you sent out for me. The letters were very nice, very polite, but there aren't any openings at those schools. Ted—about this apartment—"

Ted held the receiver away from his ear for a moment and ran a hand through his dark hair before pressing the receiver to his ear once more. "Look, Jillian," he said seriously. "This isn't easy for me to say, but I think we're going to have to start facing facts here."

"Such as?" Jillian's tone was guarded.

"Fact one: You can't get a job out here in time for this school year. Fact two: You already have a great job where you are. Fact three: I have to get an apartment within the next week or start looking for a comfortable park bench. Fact four: I can fly to Allentown on alternate weekends for free once this first month is over. Fact five—"

"Yes? Fact five?" She was crying. She wasn't making a big deal about it, but he knew she was crying. He knew just how she felt.

"Fact five:" he ended softly. "I love you, Slugger."

"I love you too, darling," she answered, sniffling.

"Then you do understand what I'm trying to say here?"

"I understand. I don't *like* it much, but I understand. It doesn't take a brain surgeon to figure out what you're saying. You want me to stay here, in Allentown, without you. Don't you?"

"No, dammit, I don't *want* you to be in Allentown while I'm in San Francisco, three thousand miles away. But it's the only solution I can think of for now. And it would only be for a while, Slugger, I promise. Only until you find a job out here."

"I might end up spending the entire school year here, Ted. Do you really want that?"

Did he want that? Ted loved Jillian, but there were times when she asked obvious questions. Of course he didn't "want that." What he wanted to do was punch a wall, or yell until his throat ached, or hop the next plane for ABE and the hell with his promotion! But he couldn't say that. He couldn't say any of that.

So he didn't say anything.

"Sorry. Dumb question," he heard Jillian mumble apologetically a moment later, when he hadn't answered her. "I'm being a baby about this, Ted, and I know it, although knowing it doesn't make any of this any easier. Will you be Steve Hammond's roommate? That is what you've been hinting at, isn't it?"

"So it's all right with you?" Ted's entire body sagged weakly in relief. Jillian was being a real brick about this thing, bless her. If only he could be with her at this moment, to kiss her, to thank her, to love her.

"I—I guess it has to be all right with me, doesn't it, darling?" she answered, her honesty and her sorrow both evident in her voice. But then she rallied. "As long as your roommate's name is really Steve—and not Stephanie!"

"Nut!" Ted returned, laughing, some of the pain around his heart easing at her graceful acceptance of their situation. "Hey, lady—have I told you yet today how very, *very* much I love you?"

He closed his eyes, believing he could almost see her beautiful, heartbreaking smile. "Not in any great detail, no," she answered, her voice suddenly husky, intimate, as if she were close beside him. "But I'd be willing to listen now if you want to whisper sweet nothings into my ear long-distance."

Ted wasn't happy about their situation, but he was relieved they had at last made a decision. He'd be in Allentown the end of next week—just a few forty-eight-hour-long days from now—and between now and then they would talk more about this odd marriage they would be living for the next six months, perhaps even a whole year.

Right now he just wanted to pretend he was a worry-free, happily married man, flirting long-distance with his wife. "Oh, really?" he teased at last, settling back in the uncomfortable sling-back chair. "Tell me, my love, would these be General Audience sweet nothings or *R*-rated sweet nothings?"

"Why don't you surprise me," Jillian said, laughing, and Ted smiled again. It *was* all right. Everything was going to be all right.

Wouldn't it?

Chapter Three

"Jill, for crying out loud! Will you please sit down? You're making me dizzy just watching you. Anyone would think you were on some sort of weird television game show. Ladies and gentlemen—can our contestant polish this lovely coffee table to within an inch of its life in less than thirty seconds? What does the winner get, Jilly—a year's supply of cleanser?"

"Very funny." Jillian hesitated only momentarily in the act of running a dust cloth over the maple coffee table, then continued with her work. "And I can't sit down, Barb," she answered, replacing the magazines on the now shining tabletop, spreading them in a fan shape the way they did in decorating magazines.

The effect was pleasing, and the magazines covered several large dents in the tabletop where, at the age of seven or so, she had absentmindedly dropped her roller skates.

"Sure you can, Jill. It's easy, actually. You just stand in front of a chair—any nearby chair will do—bend your knees and—"

"Very funny, Barb—and I *can't* sit down. Ted will be home at seven-thirty, and I still have to run the vacuum cleaner downstairs and grab a quick shower before I pick him up at the airport. Oh, why did the street department have to pick today to dig a trench in front of my house? They didn't warn me, either—didn't post signs or anything—or I wouldn't have left home with the windows open. Look at this place, Barb—I'm knee-deep in grit!"

Barbara sat back in the recliner and patted her blond curls, her dimples flashing as she smiled impishly. "Somehow I don't think Ted is going to notice whether the living room is covered with dust, or even if it's on fire when he walks in. *This* isn't the room he'll be heading for—if you get my drift."

Jillian turned away, feeling her cheeks flush with embarrassment. She knew exactly what her friend meant. The days had passed slowly, but they had passed, and she and Ted would be together tonight, Friday night, until Sunday night at six.

It was a dream come true.

And the reality of it frightened her more than she would ever let Barbara know.

Jillian told herself she was being ridiculous. How could she be nervous about being alone with Ted? He was her husband. Her beloved, loving husband.

Yet she hadn't seen him in a month. They spoke on the telephone every evening, but that wasn't the same as seeing him, being with him, having him here in their home, which had still not become his home.

Some of his clothing and shoes were beside hers in the large closet in the master bedroom, and his extra toothbrush rested alongside hers in the holder in the bathroom.

His compact discs and audio tapes were on the shelf in the living room next to her own collection. The refrigerator was stocked with his favorite foods.

But he didn't live here. He had never lived here. The only bed they had shared overnight was the king-size bed in that motel in Sea Isle City, New Jersey.

She didn't feel as if she were about to welcome her husband home. She was getting the house ready, getting herself ready, to entertain a *guest*.

"*Ummm!* Something is beginning to smell good out in the kitchen, Jill," Barbara said, bringing Jillian's mind back to both her surroundings and her friend's presence. "Could that be your world-famous throw-everything-in-one-pot onion soup, chuck roast, carrots and potatoes?"

Jillian smiled, pushing a hand through her unbound shoulder-length hair. "It could," she answered, stuffing the dust cloth in the back pocket of her shorts and picking up the can of spray wax. "But if that's a hint that you want to join us for dinner, I'm afraid you're wasting your time."

"*Moi?*" Barbara questioned, pressing her hands against her chest as if in horror at such a thought. "Oh, sure. Like I'd interrupt your second honeymoon." And then she grinned. "Although I wouldn't say no to joining you for dessert. I saw the angel food cake on the table as I came in through the kitchen. You're going to dribble whole and crushed strawberries and fresh whipped cream all over it, aren't you? Yummy!"

"Dream on," Jill said, leading the way into the kitchen where she put away the cleaning supplies. "I'll save you a piece, but for tonight, Barb, all trespassers will be shot on sight! You can join us for leftovers tomorrow at lunchtime. Oh, Lord—would you look at the time? I have to head for the shower. Barb—I'll see you tomorrow, okay? Wish me luck."

"Luck? Are you crazy?" Barbara shook her head. "You're going to see Ted soon. What do you need luck for, Jill? You should be bouncing off walls with happiness. Or is something wrong? Do you want to talk?"

Jillian rolled her eyes at her own stupidity. Why had she opened her mouth? "No, Barb, nothing's wrong and I don't need to talk. I need to take a shower, that's all. I've been run ragged by those kids at the playground all day and I haven't stopped running since I got home. I just meant that you should hope I'll get to the airport on time."

"Oh, right," Barbara answered, lifting the glass dome that covered the uniced angel food cake and picking up a few loose crumbs to toss into her mouth. "In that case, I wish you luck. They're repainting the lines on Route 22, you know. Traffic's bound to be bumper-to-bumper."

"Oh, great! That's all I need!" Jillian exploded in exasperation, already unbuttoning her short-sleeved blouse as she tore toward the stairs that led up from the dining room. "See ya, Barb!"

"Yeah, right. And don't worry, Jill. I'll run the vacuum over the rugs before I leave. Don't forget to say hello to Ted for me."

Jillian paused halfway up the stairs and leaned over the top of the thick wooden banister, grinning in relief. "Barbara McAllister—have I ever told you how very much I love you?"

"Yeah, yeah. All my married friends with dirty carpets say that," Barbara answered, walking into the dining room. "Just save me a hunk of that cake, okay?"

Ninety frantic minutes later Jillian was standing on the rooftop observation platform, watching Lombard Airways flight 2673 taxi in from the runway, her hair still faintly damp, a nick from her razor still stinging on her ankle bone beneath her stockings.

And what a ninety minutes it had been. She had only just begun to work conditioner into her hair after her shampoo when the shower water inexplicably turned tepid, then cold, so that she'd had to finish rinsing her hair while wrapped in her bathrobe, standing at the kitchen sink, pouring warmed water from the teapot over her head.

The nick from her shaver had come earlier, the first time she had cut herself shaving since she was a teenager.

And then, while rummaging wildly through the pitch-dark interior of the closet for her left shoe, which had somehow mysteriously hidden itself at the very back of the closet beneath her winter boots, the sagging wooden closet pole, never sturdy, had come crashing down on her head.

She rubbed at a spot on the back of her head, to learn that it was still tender, although the bump seemed to have gone down a little. She didn't even want to think about the condition of all their clothes, which were probably wrinkled beyond belief—for she had quickly decided that she couldn't take the time necessary to rehang the pole and had only firmly closed the closet door on the mess.

By the time she had dressed herself in a brand new pale yellow culotte skirt and a matching yellow-and-white striped cotton summer sweater she had begun to believe the gods had cursed her.

She had known it for a fact when, after three frantic tries, her usually fairly reliable car wouldn't start. She had to go back into the house and hunt up the keys to Ted's car, which had a standard shift—and she hadn't driven a standard shift in four years.

But she had made it. She had made it with at least five minutes to spare, although she would probably never know how. Pushing her windblown hair out of her eyes, she turned and made her way back down the stairs to the arrivals section of the terminal, her heart pounding in her throat as she wondered—crazily, she knew—if she'd recognize Ted when he came through the door beyond the metal detector.

There was already a small crowd gathered behind the ropes; mothers and children, an elderly couple holding a stuffed teddy bear as if awaiting a visiting grandchild, a nervous-looking teenager holding a bouquet of roses and a tired-looking young woman holding an infant while a two-year-old repeatedly tugged at her skirt hem.

They were all waiting for someone important to arrive, someone who had come to join them over miles and miles of separation, to become a part of a whole that had been splintered, either for a few days or—in Jillian's case—for an entire month, an eternity of time.

Maybe she should have brought flowers? No, that was ridiculous! What would Ted do with a bouquet of roses? Why was she so nervous? She had to get a grip on herself! If only the water would be hot again once they got home, for surely Ted would want a shower. He didn't want roses. He wanted a shower. A *hot* shower.

She bit her bottom lip, wondering if she looked all right, if she looked as Ted remembered her. She was more tanned, she knew, for she was spending her days in the sun, either monitoring games on the playground or watching the youngest children in the wading pool. Her hair might even be a little bit longer. She was aware that she was overdue for a haircut and longed to have it all cut short for the summer.

But she hadn't wanted to radically change her hairstyle while Ted was gone. It would be like doing something behind his back.

And then the double doors at the end of the hallway opened. People began to straggle down the long ramp into the more open area—and the time for all her nervous thoughts had run out.

She stood on tiptoe, leaning forward, as if that would help her see beyond the family of five that had come through the double doors first, followed by a heavyset man struggling with at least thirty-five pounds of assorted carry-on luggage.

And then she saw him.

Handsomely dressed in his dark blue flight uniform—for he had told her he would be leaving straight from class—he strode down the ramp confidently, his head held high, his cap tipped back on his dark hair, a wide grin splitting his gorgeous tanned face.

Theodore J-for-Joseph Hackett. Ted. Her Ted. *Her husband.*

Jillian stood very still, her bottom lip beginning to wobble as tears stung at her eyes. How could she have believed she could forget what he looked like— how wonderful he looked. His features were imprinted on her heart. Indelible. *Forever.*

"Slugger!"

She raised her hand to wave at him as he immediately broke into a trot, brushing past the heavyset man with all the luggage, neatly sidestepping a small child who lagged behind her parents before he vaulted over the leather-covered rope stanchion that separated the arrival area from the visitors area.

He stopped just in front of her, smiling, wordlessly shaking his head, then said again, softly, caressingly, "God, Jilly, how I've *missed* you!"

A small sob tore from her throat as he dropped his small black suitcase. He gathered her into his arms and, lifting her fully off the floor as his mouth came down on hers, he kissed her passionately, hungrily, as if he would never let her go.

She kissed him back, even as he began to move in a small circle, round and round, as if they were dancing to music only they could hear.

She clung to him even as his hat fell to the floor; even as grandparents greeted their grandchild; even as the harried housewife sniffed in cynical observation as she pushed past Ted and Jillian to hear her husband complain about the food on the flight and ask what was for dinner; even as the little girl with the Raggedy Ann doll asked her mother "What are those two people doing, Mommy? Is he hurting her?"

Actually, it was this last dose of reality that finally brought Jillian back to earth after her marvelous encounter with heaven, and she reluctantly pushed herself free of Ted, who allowed her feet to touch the floor once more.

But he didn't let her go far.

He picked up his small suitcase, handed it to her, then pressed his uniform hat onto her head at a jaunty angle. Slipping a proprietorial arm around her shoulders, he then led her toward the luggage carousel where his weekender was waiting, using his free hand to snatch it up before steering the two of them toward the exit.

"Miss me?" he asked, stopping just outside the door to kiss her again before she could answer.

"Maybe a little," she teased a moment later, tossing him the keys to the car that was just inside the parking lot—the only break she had gotten was finding a parking spot near the door. "Now and then. Mostly, I've kept myself busy."

"Busy? Oh, really? That sounds ominous. And just how have you been keeping yourself busy, Mrs. Hackett?" Ted unlocked the passenger door and threw his luggage into the back seat before Jillian, removing the hat, slid into the front bucket seat.

She waited impatiently, idly toying with the stiff brim of his hat until he was sitting in the driver's seat and had inserted the key in the ignition, before answering.

"Oh, this and that. A little bit of this, a little more of that. Working at the playground, planting flowers, mowing the lawn, making homemade angel food cake—" she grinned at him "—and changing the sheets on our bed."

His hands stilled on the steering wheel as he turned to look at her. "You didn't get rid of the pink flowered ones, did you? I know we men aren't supposed to like that stuff, but they've figured in a major part of my best daydreams for a whole month."

Jillian felt herself blushing again, as she had done earlier with Barbara. But this time she knew it was not from nervousness or embarrassment. "Oh, really? I think I'd like to hear about these daydreams of yours, Mr. Hackett. Tell me," she added boldly, "did I happen to figure in any of them?"

He slid his arm across the back of her bucket seat, his grin intriguingly wicked and his dimple in evidence in his right cheek. When his mouth was only a heartbeat from hers he whispered huskily, "Figure in them? Slugger, you were the star!"

Jillian's eyelids fluttered closed as his warm lips claimed hers and she gave herself up to his kisses once more, wondering how on earth she had ever believed there had been anything to be worried about.

Her husband was home.

Chapter Four

"I do love you, darling. And do you want to know *why* I love you? It's because you're so very, *very* good with your hands."

Ted, who was leaning over the engine compartment of Jillian's car making a final corrective adjustment on the newly installed fan belt, tilted his head and looked up at his wife.

Her elbows were resting on the top of the left front fender, her chin propped in her hands. Her coppery hair was hanging freely onto her shoulders, teased by the slight breeze and warmed by the late morning sun.

She was wearing a small, "I-know-just-what-you're-thinking-and-so-am-I" smile, a hot pink halter top, a pair of skimpy white shorts and little else.

Her smile broadened, showing him the slight dimples on either side of her full lips, the same enticing dimples he had kissed last night. He had kissed her dimples, her full mouth, the faint birthmark on the underside of her left breast—every sweet, glorious inch of her.

"Lady, you sure do pick your times!" he said at last in mingled exasperation and desire, shaking his head, so that one long lock of inky dark hair fell forward onto his forehead.

"Why, thank you, darling. I try," she replied airily before pushing herself away from the fender and walking—slowly, oh, so slowly—up the brick path to the back door of the house, turning at the last minute to throw him a come-hither look that nearly had him bumping his head on the car hood in his haste to follow after her.

Ted wiped his greasy hands on the faded jeans that fit him like a second skin. He was in a hurry to shower in the small stall that unfortunately would not allow for a repeat of their romp in the motel room shower in Sea Isle City. Afterward he'd take up where he and Jillian had left off at approximately three that morning.

In their bed.

She had been a wonder to him from the moment they had stepped inside the back door last night, playing at the same time the roles of both loving, devoted wife and sweet enchantress. They had remained in the kitchen only long enough to put the dinner she'd prepared in the refrigerator. They hadn't gotten around to eating it until hours later. A *lot* of hours later.

Even then they hadn't been very hungry, merely picking at the main course, then tarrying over dessert, Jillian feeding him strawberries one at a time as they lounged on the living room carpet, his head in her lap as they listened to the stereo. In turn, he had fed her small sips of champagne as they had nibbled at the spongy angel food cake.

The reality of his homecoming had, in Ted's biased opinion, sure beaten the hell out of any fantasy he could have created in his mind during those long, lonely nights in San Francisco.

He passed by Jillian in the kitchen just as she was preparing to slide a container of leftover roast beef, potatoes and carrots into the microwave and looked up at the clock to see that it was already twelve-thirty.

"Hungry, darling?" she asked, pushing some buttons on the microwave before turning to him.

He ran his gaze from her eyes, down to her bare toes, and back again to her face. "Hungry? Actually, I'm *starving*," he said, so that there could be no question as to what he meant.

She gave a toss of her head, sending her blunt-cut shoulder-length hair swinging around her cheeks. She batted her eyelashes furiously as she pressed a hand to the modest swell of cleavage that rose above the halter top. "Why, land o'goshen, sir, I do believe you just might have amorous designs on little ole me."

"Damn straight," Ted replied, deciding to forego his shower and their lunch. He took two steps in her direction before he looked down at his grease-coated hands.

He needed a shower, a good hot shower, to remove the grease. He stopped, pointing one all-blackened finger in her direction. "Don't move! I'll be back before that buzzer goes off."

"Is that a threat or a promise?" Jillian asked, leaning back against the countertop, grinning.

"It's a vow," Ted answered, looking back at her over his shoulder as he headed for the stairs in the dining room. "A sub-vow, actually. You'll find it listed somewhere under the general heading that begins with the words 'to love and to cherish.' And I'm the kind of guy who takes his vows seriously!"

He was already stripping off his black tank top with the words "Love is better in Sea Isle City" emblazoned on the back in neon green letters as he stepped into the small, old-fashioned hall bathroom.

He rolled the shirt into a ball and aimed it in the general direction of the hamper, then stepped out of his jeans before reaching behind the glass shower door and turning on the faucets.

Three minutes later he was humming a top-ten rock tune whose title escaped him as he worked shampoo into his hair, warm water pouring over his shoulders to run sleekly down his well muscled body.

He was happy, he was in love, and life was grand.

Or at least it was until the shower water turned tepid, then cold. Stone cold.

His eyes squeezed shut to keep shampoo out of them, Ted groped blindly for the faucets, trying to adjust the temperature. It was no use. There simply was no more hot water. Rinsing his hair and body under the needle-sharp cold spray didn't do a heck of a lot for his libido, not to mention his general mood.

"Rotten, lousy, *stupid* old house!" His fingertips still faintly grease stained, he shut off the faucets, slammed open the glass shower door, wrapped a bath towel around his waist and stomped to the bedroom to locate some clean clothes.

Having dressed this morning in the only extra clothing he had brought with him from San Francisco, he now quite naturally turned to the closet to locate a pair of tan slacks and, because Jillian had told him she liked it, his navy pullover.

What he found when he opened the door to the closet caused a hissed curse to escape through his compressed lips. All his clothes, all of Jillian's clothes, were lying on the floor, still on their hangers.

The closet pole, an ancient and slightly warped-looking wooden contraption, lay on top of the clothing, and he could see that one of its large metal brackets had worked loose from the wall, allowing the pole to fall.

He turned away from the closet to unearth clean underwear from his suitcase. "Jillian!" he bellowed, hastily rubbing himself dry before slamming the towel in the direction of the closet. "Hey—*Jillian!* Would you come up here, please?"

She joined him just as he had zipped closed a pair of khaki shorts and was beginning to comb through his damp hair. "What's up, Ted? Are you trying to set the new North American record for quick showers? The microwave buzzer hasn't even gone off yet."

"I ran out of hot water," he said in explanation, wishing he could be in a better mood. But he couldn't. It was only Saturday afternoon, and already he'd had to fix one busted fan belt. Was he going to have to spend the rest of the day fooling around with a broken water heater? And what about the clothes pole in the closet? Was he the new weekend handyman?

He put thought into speech before she could reply to his terse explanation about his swift shower. "What in hell happened in the closet, Slugger? Were you doing chin-ups in there?"

"Omigosh, the closet!" Her hands flew to her cheeks and her green eyes grew wide. "I forgot! The pole fell when I was getting ready to pick you up last night. I would have gone into the closet last night for a nightgown—but we never did get around to nightgowns, did we? And then this morning, well, I keep my shorts and tops in a dresser drawer—so I just never opened the closet. Oh, Ted. Everything will be a *mess!* I'll be ironing for *days!*"

Ted covered his mouth to hide his smile at her obvious distress. "Life's a bummer, Slugger," he said, his ill humor vanishing, to be replaced by genuine sympathy. "But at least it'll keep you home nights. I can't say that I'd enjoy being alone in San Francisco, thinking about you running around here in outfits like this one."

He kissed the tip of her ear. "Don't worry, honey. It will only take me a couple of minutes to fix the pole. I guess adding my clothing just proved too much for it."

She nodded, then leaned her head into his chest. "And the water heater? It gave me some trouble yesterday, too, although it was fine for you last night and for my shower this morning—at least it sort of was. I should have let you shower first today, instead of hogging all the hot water for myself. I'm so sorry, Ted. I imagine we need to install a new heating element or something."

Her voice was very small, as if she had hated to bring up the subject. He knew how she felt. He hated to even *hear* her bringing up the subject.

"Or something," he agreed, dropping a kiss on her hair, then taking hold of her slim shoulders and turning her toward the door to the hallway. "But for now, let's eat. We'll play happy homemakers after lunch."

She turned her head and looked up at him, pouting, so that he could not help but concentrate on her full, moist lips. "I thought we were going to play *house* after lunch," she said quietly. "You're only going to be here until tomorrow afternoon, Ted. I don't want to spend all of that time putting bandages on this old house. I installed a new heating element by myself a couple of years ago—but I guess this is one job that can't wait until Monday."

Ted laughed out loud. "Honey—I've taken enough cold showers this past month. We are going to *fix* that water heater today."

The sound of the kitchen screen door slamming shut echoed inside the house. "Knock, knock! Hey—is anybody home?"

Jillian paused on the second step from the top of the stairs, rolling her eyes as she lifted a finger to her lips. "It's Barbara," she whispered conspiratorially. "I forgot. Yesterday, in a moment of weakness, I invited her to join us for lunch today. If we're quiet, maybe she'll go away. I love Barb—really, I do, but—"

"Hey, guys!" Barbara called from somewhere downstairs, probably the kitchen. "The buzzer just went off on the microwave. Everything smells delicious. Were you still planning to have lunch, or do you think you can live on love?"

Ted sighed fatalistically and motioned for Jillian to lead the way downstairs. "Barb's got a point, Slugger. We do have to eat."

"Here you are!" Barbara said as Ted and Jillian entered the kitchen to see their next-door neighbor setting the table—with *three* plates. "You know, I'd be the last one to interrupt your romantic weekend but—" She turned back toward the table, at last looking in their direction. "Wow! Jill, you said he was built, but—*wow!*"

Ted realized that he was clad in only his khaki shorts, exposing his tanned chest to Barbara's to say the least *interested* inspection. Her admiration did a lot for his ego, even if he was an old married man, and he decided that maybe sharing their potluck lunch with Barbara wasn't *entirely* a bad thing.

"Thanks, Barb," he said, pulling out a chair and sitting down. "Jill," he continued teasingly, smiling as he watched his wife open the microwave and pull the container from its interior, "you never told me you've been bragging about my body. First my brains, and now this!" He leaned backward in the chair, tipping it back on two legs. "Gee, I might begin to get a big head."

Jillian placed the container in the middle of the table. "Don't worry, honey, I also told Barb what a slob you are," she said sweetly.

"Me?" Ted feigned shock, although he knew that his dirty clothes were, at this very moment, draped all over the bathroom and his wet towel was lying on the bedroom carpet. "Gosh, Slugger, I'm shocked. Really shocked. Why, anyone would think I had a whole *closetful* of clothing just lying around on the floor."

"Very *un*funny, darling," Jillian said, plunking three tall ice-cube-filled glasses on the tabletop before retrieving a pitcher of homemade iced tea from the refrigerator. "Barb—would you like to get the salad bowls?"

Barbara retrieved three bowls from the cabinet, before seating herself in the chair across from Ted, so that he couldn't help noticing that for all her air of being a welcome guest the young woman was looking decidedly uncomfortable.

It had to be difficult, this business of having your lifelong friend suddenly change into a married woman—even if for a while at least it was only going to be for alternate weekends.

"Barbara," he said as Jillian lifted the lid from the container of leftover roast and potatoes and aromatic steam escaped into the air, "have I told you how grateful I am that Jill has you to turn to now that I've been transferred? I really feel much better knowing that you and your mother are right next door."

Barbara blushed a flattering pink to the roots of her curly blond hair. "Oh, that's okay, Ted, honestly. I mean, Mom and I have been watching out for Jill ever since her mother and stepfather left for Barcelona. I'm just glad Jill didn't go with you to—whoops!"

Jillian paused in raising a forkful of potato to her mouth and smiled at her friend. "That's all right, Barb. I know you didn't mean that the way it sounded. Besides, this separation is only temporary." She turned to Ted. "Isn't it, darling?"

"Right!" Ted answered brightly. Too brightly. And he knew it. Last night might have seemed like an extension of their honeymoon, but today reality had come crashing back—too soon. Much too soon.

Ted didn't remember much of the conversation that went on around him for the remainder of the meal. He was distracted by thoughts of Jillian—and continuing the lovemaking that had been interrupted by Barbara's arrival.

After Barbara had gone, Ted helped Jillian clear the table of dessert plates and coffee cups, while water to wash the dishes heated on the stove.

"Shall I try to make up for my slovenly ways and wash these dishes for you?" Ted asked, as he placed the last dirty cup into the sink filled with hot, sudsy water.

"I can do it, darling," Jillian answered, lifting a handful of soap suds and smiling as she slowly spread the bubbles across his chest. "Besides, I was only teasing before. I love you just the way you are," she ended, dabbing the last bit of bubbles on the end of his nose.

Ted stepped closer, grinning down at her. "In San Francisco, I always let my dishes soak in hot water while I watch the news," he said, tipping up her chin with the knuckle of his index finger.

Her green eyes shone with mischief. "Oh, really? How terribly *inventive* of you, Ted. Are you suggesting we go into the living room and turn on the all-news station?"

He quickly slid one arm around Jillian's back and the other beneath her knees, lifting her high against his bare, still slightly soapy chest. *"Bzzz!"* he hissed into her ear, imitating a game show's mechanical buzzer. "Sorry. Wrong answer, Mrs. Hackett, but thank you for playing our game. We do offer some lovely parting gifts—"

She laid her head against his shoulder as he exited the kitchen, on his way toward the staircase. "Oh, Ted, that's such an *old* line. But I love it. And I love you!"

Later that day they bought an element for the water heater at a home-supply store located at a neighboring shopping mall.

Much later that day.

Chapter Five

Ted caught the jump seat—the name given to the small fold-down cockpit seat—once more in July and then again the second week in August.

By now he had flown the San Francisco-to-Hawaii route several times, although his position was only that of an observer, and according to him, "I might as well have been stuck back with the rest of the passengers, watching the movie. But soon, Slugger—soon I'll be in the first officer's seat."

Each time he had come home, Jillian had met him at the airport with a smile and a kiss, and they had gone back to the small house on Nineteenth Street to spend two glorious days together.

They had cooked one-and-a-half-inch-thick steaks on the backyard grill, gone on a day trip to Philadelphia, fed the ducks at nearby Muhlenberg Lake, spent an afternoon sliding down the chutes and swimming in the wave pool at Dorney Park's Wild Water Kingdom and had taken in an outdoor movie at the local Shankweiler's Drive-in.

And thankfully both the house and Jillian's car had cooperated splendidly, so that the toolbox remained neatly tucked away in the basement stairwell for the entire two months.

In short, they had spent their weekends as if they were small vacations from the realities of everyday life which in a way they were.

But now the summer was officially drawing to a close, and the day after Labor Day Jillian would enter a classroom for the first time as a full-time teacher. She was nervous and excited all at once. When Ted called her late Wednesday night and suggested she spend the long three-day holiday weekend in San Francisco with him she had a lot of trouble making her enthusism sound convincing.

"Me? San Francisco?" she repeated, her voice squeaking just a bit in her dismay. "That—that sounds lovely, darling." She closed her eyes and read down mental lists of chores she had planned for the two of them this weekend as well as her private to-do list, to prepare her for the start of classes.

"Yeah, that's what I thought," Ted said, his voice traveling to her over the phone wires. "Steve just told me tonight that he's planning to fly home to Houston to be with his folks for the holiday. We'll have the whole place to ourselves."

"The whole place, huh?" Jillian sat back on the kitchen chair, looking at the curtains she'd wanted to wash that weekend. It had always been a family tradition to start fall housecleaning over the Labor Day weekend, then spend the holiday itself at the Lehigh Parkway picnic grounds with Barbara's family.

Even after her mother remarried and moved to Spain with Jillian's stepfather and even after Barbara's mother was widowed, Barbara and Jillian had continued the tradition, and Barbara had been over just that afternoon helping her to plan the menu.

And it wasn't as if Ted didn't know about their plans, gosh darn it all, anyway, for Jillian had told him last night on the phone.

"Jill? Honey?" Ted's voice sounded slightly apprehensive. "You do want to come, don't you? I mean, I don't hear any sounds of you jumping up and down with glee or anything."

She sat forward on the chair, leaning her elbows on the table. "Of course I want to come!" she exclaimed quickly, knowing she was lying. Ted had been waxing poetic about San Francisco for weeks now and she couldn't help feeling that he wanted her to come out there so he could do his best Chamber of Commerce sell job on the area. He was especially fond of a place called Mill Valley and some houses located somewhere within view of the ocean.

She was certain the area was beautiful—which, she was also certain, was the reason she didn't want to see it. They had married with the agreement that Allentown would be their home. It wasn't fair of Ted to go changing the ground rules.

"Then it's all settled! You'll fly out Friday at one—you did say the playground staff gets off at noon on Friday, didn't you—lay over for a couple of minutes at O'Hare in Chicago and land in San Francisco in great time. You'll have to fly standby, but there won't be any problem. The flight is rarely ever full, even on holidays. You'll arrive back in Allentown around ten-thirty Monday night, in plenty of time to get a good night's sleep before your first day of school."

With the cordless phone pressed to her ear, Jillian rose from her chair and began pacing the kitchen. *Ten-thirty? Was the man insane? She'd be lucky if she got to bed before one in the morning!* "How efficient," she said, knowing she was in danger of grinding her teeth.

Ted couldn't have worked jet lag and the problems of traveling through three time zones into his time schedule for her, she realized ruefully, but she wasn't going to mention it—at least not now, when he sounded so happy. "It sounds like you've got everything set, almost as if I'd already said yes."

"Well, yeah—sort of," Ted answered, his tone so hurt that Jillian rolled her eyes, knowing she was being petty. Ted had planned what he believed would be a lovely surprise, and she was acting as if he'd made her an appointment for root-canal work at the dentist.

"What should I pack?" she asked, forcing a happy note into her voice.

"Just your sweet self, Slugger," Ted answered happily, so that Jillian knew he was completely oblivious to the fact that she was going to have to do some fancy footwork not to hurt Barbara's feelings. "And maybe some of that perfume I brought you last time."

Jillian smiled, remembering not only the perfume, but the way he had *helped* her dab it at the pulse of her throat, her nape, the small of her back....

"You've got a deal," she said. "Now tell me those flight times again so I can write them down."

The sun shining down brilliantly on the Pacific Ocean was stunning—a perfect display for Jillian's first visit to the West Coast. As they drove in from the airport, Ted could tell by Jillian's expression that she was impressed.

He supposed he should be happy that something had finally worked out as planned.

Jillian had arrived in San Francisco a full two hours late, thanks to a mechanical problem with the airplane at O'Hare, and had come off the plane hungry, tired and looking just a tad green around the gills, for there had been some turbulence over the Rockies.

And so, all things considered, Jillian's flight hadn't been a particularly auspicious beginning to what Ted most sincerely hoped would be a milestone weekend in their young marriage.

He had whisked her into Steve's car and back to the apartment, stopping along the way at the drive-through window of a fast-food restaurant for some hamburgers and fries.

His apartment, located in the Mission District, was near the water. The ocean couldn't be seen from any of the windows—unless you stood on the corner of the bathtub, tilted your head just so and peered intently to the left—but he was proud of the place and couldn't wait to show it off.

He also couldn't wait to hold Jillian in his arms, to kiss her, to take her to the bed he had occupied alone these past months.

But, he was to remember often in the next hour, even the best laid plans don't always fall neatly into place.

Upon returning to the apartment they were greeted by Steve, who had somehow managed to miss his flight. Ted could hardly introduce Jillian to Steve, wolf down a couple of hamburgers and then in caveman style whisk his gorgeous wife off to the privacy of his bedroom.

Sure he *wanted* to, but he knew he couldn't.

So in the end Jillian—who had announced that her stomach wasn't quite up to a greasy fast-food feast—handed her meal to Steve and the three of them talked until it was time for Steve to leave for the airport again. Ted and Jillian drove him to the airport and then returned to watch the tail end of a glorious sunset at the beach.

"Like it?" Ted asked now, pulling Jillian against him as sea gulls swooped along the water's edge and split the air with their raucous cries. "Growing up in half a dozen different places throughout the Midwest, moving every couple of years when my dad was transferred, I just can't seem to get enough of watching the ocean."

"It's beautiful all right," Jillian answered, then twisted her head slightly to look back at the Mission District. "Isn't this the area that was so badly hit during the last big earthquake? Here in the Mission District and over in Oakland?"

"Yes," Ted answered, wishing Jillian hadn't remembered that particular piece of San Francisco's history. He hadn't had a place he could call home in a long time, not since his parents had died, and he had only been stationed in Allentown for a couple of years. Hardly long enough to put down real roots.

San Francisco had an appeal he couldn't quite put a name to, but somehow the place had already begun to feel like home to him. He wanted Jillian to concentrate on the beauty of the area and not dwell on anything she might twist into a drawback to the place.

"But the district has recovered from the earthquake and the occasional earth tremor isn't all that discouraging when you consider all the benefits of San Francisco. There are some great people living out here, Slugger. And besides it's such a beautiful place and the city is so alive, so full of culture, so—"

"So beautiful," Jillian finished for him, smiling up into his face, although her smile seemed strained. "And I agree, darling. The whole area is charming. Your apartment is charming. Steve is charming. And I'm willing to bet that Mill Valley is even *more* charming. You are going to give me the grand tour tomorrow, aren't you?"

Ted took her hand and led her back toward the parked car. He should have known that Jillian had already figured out what he was up to. For weeks now he'd been sounding like a used-car salesman looking for a big commission whenever he spoke of San Francisco.

"I'm not being very subtle, am I, Slugger?" he said as he helped her into the passenger seat of Steve's low-slung sports car.

"Actually—no," she answered, then waited until he was seated behind the steering wheel to add, "but I can understand your enthusiasm. San Francisco really is wonderful. It's just—it's just that—"

"It's just that we'd already agreed on Allentown once I'm allowed to pick my permanent base and

Allentown is also wonderful. Of course, it doesn't snow or sleet in San Francisco," he couldn't resist pointing out as he slipped the key into the ignition.

"I *like* the snow," Jillian answered shortly, turning so that she was facing front in the car as he drove the five long blocks to the parking garage behind the apartment. "I've *always* liked the snow."

"And the sleet? And the freezing rain?" Ted asked as they made their way into the apartment.

"I adore them both," Jillian answered, squeezing the obvious fib from between clenched teeth as she passed by him and entered the living area. "And Allentown isn't exactly a cultural desert, you know. We have plenty of live theater, and an art museum and all that sort of thing, and we're only a short trip away from New York City and the Jersey shore. Sun*rises* over the *Atlantic* Ocean are impressive, too, you know."

Ted tossed the ring of car keys onto a small table and joined Jillian at the sliding-glass doors that overlooked the street below. She was standing so very straight as she stared through the glass at San Francisco, like a soldier at attention—or a frightened child staring down a threatening bully—that his heart went out to her.

Their marriage hadn't exactly been easy so far, with both of them having to deal with a lot of changes they hadn't expected. Jillian couldn't have foreseen a commuter marriage and she certainly hadn't asked for a husband who wanted to uproot her and move the two of them three thousand miles away from the only home she'd ever known.

He leaned down, nuzzling the soft skin at her nape. "Are we having our first argument, Mrs. Hackett?" he asked facetiously, deliberately allowing his breath to tickle her ear.

She turned away from the sliding-glass doors, slipping her arms around his waist as she looked up into his face, so that he could see the faint glimmer of tears in her eyes. "I hope not, Ted," she said as she pressed her cheek against his chest. "I'm sorry. I know I'm being a witch, but I thought we were all decided about living in Allentown. I mean, it has a history for me. It has—"

"Traditions, and you're a stickler for tradition," he ended for her, as he began guiding her toward the bedroom. "We might only be married for a couple of months, Slugger, but that's one thing I've learned about you. Roast beef is reserved for homecomings and Sunday dinners, you must sleep on the right side of the bed, your dad's old recliner has to be in the left-front corner of the living room and the world would end tomorrow if you didn't brush your teeth after every meal."

She gave him a playful punch in the ribs as she left him to sit on the edge of the bed, which was where he had wanted to see her ever since she had deplaned. "You make me sound so predictable, Ted. I'm surprised you didn't mention that I always begin fall housecleaning over Labor Day weekend."

He kicked off his loafers and joined her on the bed, plopping his long frame down heavily, so that the springs squeaked and Jillian had to brace herself to remain upright.

"I forgot about that one," he admitted teasingly, gently pushing her down onto the bedspread. "Or maybe I intentionally blocked it out. Housecleaning! Is that some foreign word?"

Jillian laughed. "Only to people like you, darling, who believe that houses are inhabited by friendly little gremlins who tippytoe out of their hiding places in the middle of the night to hang up the clothes you drop on the floor, fold up used newspapers and carry your dirty dishes into the kitchen."

He began opening the small covered buttons that lined the front of her blouse. "You mean there's no such animal? Maybe that explains why Steve and I spent most of last night running a bulldozer around this place, trying to clean it up for your visit."

"That could be your problem, darling," she said, raising a hand to run her fingers through his hair. "But the apartment looks fine to me—although I haven't seen much of the kitchen yet, have I?"

"Just don't open any containers in the refrigerator, Slugger. You wouldn't want to press your luck." He trailed his fingers over the silky tanned skin exposed above her lacy camisole as he gently pressed his lips against the pulse point at the base of her throat.

"Besides—didn't you see that dead horse in the living room? Or did the clutter camouflage it enough?" he asked teasingly, then changed the subject, raising his head to look deeply into her wonderful green eyes.

"You don't know how I've longed to see you like this, Slugger," he said seriously, his voice grown slightly husky with love and need. "Right here with me... in my bed... in my arms... the way married people are supposed to be."

Quick tears shone in her eyes once more as a strangely sad smile tugged at the corners of her mouth. "I know, darling," she said, pulling him down so that their lips were only a heartbeat apart. "Believe me—I know."

"I love you, Jill. Really love you."

"I know that, too," she answered, insinuating her body even more intimately against his. "Now why don't you shut up and show me."

He was immediately obedient.

Chapter Six

Jillian arose early the next morning, drawn out of bed by the sound of sea gulls screeching somewhere off in the distance. She grabbed clean clothing from her suitcase and quietly headed for the shower. Ted deserved a few more hours of sleep. After all, she thought, smiling, they'd had a long night.

Being serenaded by sea gulls wasn't an *entirely* unpleasant way to wake up, she concluded after she had showered and dressed. Just different. She was more used to hearing robins, finches and the occasional crow outside her bedroom window at home.

She stood on the small balcony that led off the living room of the second-floor apartment, a steaming cup of coffee in her hands, watching the Mission District stretch itself awake.

San Francisco—at least the little she had seen of it—*was* beautiful, just as she had told Ted. It would be a delightful place to live and work. And Ted Hackett certainly wasn't the only person to think so. After all, California was the most populous state in the Union—as Ted had delicately pointed out to her last night.

She smiled as she remembered his enthusiasm when he spoke about San Francisco. *Delicately?* Hardly. He had been about as subtle in his sales pitch as a door-to-door salesman. All that had been lacking was a handful of colorful brochures showing the advantages to be enjoyed if she chose to purchase his "product."

There was a large canvas floor cushion on the balcony and Jillian sat on it cross-legged as she sipped her coffee and peered down on the street through the wrought-iron railing.

In the space of five minutes, fourteen joggers—she counted them!—passed by her down the street, all of them probably heading in the direction of the ocean. They were all tall and slim and gloriously tan. Most of them, both male and female, were young and blond, and they all looked wonderfully fit.

And all the women seemed to have long, straight legs that reached all the way to their necks!

So this is what Ted wakes up to every morning, she thought, the cooling coffee suddenly bitter on her tongue. *The "beautiful" people. California people. The California life-style.*

No wonder Ted was so darned enthused about the place.

"And no wonder I feel so left out," she mused aloud, rising to go back inside and see if there were any eggs and bacon for breakfast.

The kitchen was the small, modern galley sort of affair, with white-on-white cabinets and appliances, including a dishwasher, which was one appliance Jillian truly envied Ted for having—especially since he had already admitted he didn't use the thing.

All in all, it was a pleasant place to live. Even though the building itself was about fifty years old, the interior of the furnished apartment was comfortably modern, without seeming sterile.

The large living room was decorated in beiges and golds, with splashes of blue and green in the upholstered furniture, and the dining area just off the galley kitchen sported a glass-topped table and four blue-cushioned rattan chairs.

There were two bedrooms, Ted's and Steve's, and although Jillian had only seen one of them, she imagined that they were similarly furnished, the dressers and chests painted white, with the queen-size beds covered in blue-and-green striped bedspreads.

In short, the apartment was lovely. The neighborhood was lovely. Steve seemed to be a very nice guy. Ted couldn't help but be comfortable.

"So why do I wish the apartment was a positive hellhole and Ted was miserable and unable to cope and couldn't wait to get back to Allentown?" she asked herself, opening the refrigerator and peering inside after noticing that there were no eggs in the handy-dandy egg holder located inside the door.

The light inside the refrigerator was burned out so that she had to nearly stick her head inside in order to take a quick inventory of its contents. There wasn't much to see beyond a quart of milk, a tub of soft margarine and a half dozen cans of iced tea.

She opened the meat drawer and stepped back when the odor of spoiled bologna assaulted her nostrils, then swiftly shut the door. Ted hadn't been kidding when he said she shouldn't "look too closely" at the results of his housekeeping.

A quick check of the small freezer revealed a quart of butter-pecan ice cream, a dozen microwavable frozen dinners and four ice trays—one of them completely empty. She didn't have much better luck as she opened cabinet doors and found four boxes of cereal, a box of instant mashed potatoes and three cans of tuna fish.

Jillian shook her head, wondering how on earth Ted and Steve managed to exist without good food. But then just as she was about to become angry at the thought that Ted might be spending half his salary eating in expensive restaurants, her features and her mood brightened.

Grabbing twenty dollars from her purse she looked around for Ted's keys to the front door and then quietly slipped out of the apartment, intent on locating a corner grocery store where she could purchase some groceries for a good breakfast and maybe even a chicken and some vegetables to prepare for dinner.

Ted might have sun and fun and long-legged joggers, but there was one thing California couldn't give him, and that was Jillian's good home cooking!

She had just descended to the first-floor landing and was turning to skip down the last flight to the ground floor when the door of the apartment just beneath Ted's opened and a young woman stepped into the hallway, already in the act of bending down to retrieve her morning newspaper.

"Well, hi, there," the woman said brightly, straightening as she smiled at Jillian. "You've got to be Jill. You're just as Ted has described you—and he has described you ad infinitum to anyone who cares to listen, I might add. Beautiful day, isn't it, even for the last weekend in August? Are you heading out for a run? I'm Nicky, by the way—Nicky Hunter."

Jillian returned the woman's smile as she extended her right hand, saying, "Jill Hackett. It's a pleasure to meet you. So, you know Ted?" It was a stupid question, especially considering the fact that Nicky had already said as much, but it was the only thing Jillian could think of to say as she tried not to stare at the woman.

Nicky Hunter was gorgeous! Standing an inch taller than Jillian herself, Nicky had porcelain white skin, midnight black hair and shining blue eyes. *Add those ruby red lips of hers, while you're at it,* Jillian thought somewhat nastily. *Anybody would think Nicky Hunter was auditioning for the latest film version of the story of Snow White.*

And Nicky Hunter, this gorgeous, breathtakingly beautiful creature, lived only one short flight of steps away from Ted. From *her* Ted. Her husband of only a little more than three months; her husband whom she had seen for a total of fifteen days in those more than three months. Did Jillian like San Francisco?

Oh, sure. Right. She just *adored* the place.

But Nicky was talking, pushing one slender, well-shaped hand through her below-the-shoulder-length ebony hair, her wide smile showing both rows of beautiful, straight white teeth. "This apartment building is almost strictly Lombard people, Jill," she said informatively. "I think there are eight of us, or at least there were the last time I counted noses. Captains on temporary assignment, first officers, navigators, flight attendants, trainees. Didn't Ted tell you that?"

Had Ted told her that? Jillian supposed so, although the information must have slipped her mind. Nicky must be one of the flight attendants, she decided, not stopping to realize that she was simplistically categorizing the woman by sex rather than considering her qualifications.

"Yes—yes, I think he did," she said quickly. "I'm happy to meet you. I hate to rush away, really I do, but I was just about to head out on an emergency visit to a grocery store. The cupboards are pretty bare upstairs. Tell me, Nicky, do you know of any stores that are within walking distance?"

Nicky laughed out loud, a soft, tinkling sound that was utterly feminine and without guile. "Those guys," she said, shaking her head. "The pizza-delivery man makes so many trips up those steps that I believe the carpet is beginning to wear thin. There is a small grocery store two blocks east of here, but maybe I can save you a trip. I've got wheat germ, kiwi fruit, skim milk and some delicious blueberry yogurt. Want to borrow some?"

Wheat germ? Blueberry yogurt? *Oh, yeah,* Jillian thought, *I'm in California, all right.* "Um, no thanks, Nicky. But thank you for offering. I do try to watch our cholesterol, but today is sort of special, you understand, so I thought we'd indulge in some sinfully dangerous panfried bacon and even a couple of scrambled eggs."

"Sounds yummy," Nicky answered, already turning to reenter her apartment. "I'd do the same thing—if I knew how to cook. I'm afraid I never learned."

Jillian frowned at this seeming contradiction. "You've never learned how to cook? But doesn't that make your job difficult? I mean, as a stew—that is, as a flight attendant, isn't it important that you at least know something about food preparation?"

Nicky turned back to Jillian, resting her shoulder against the doorjamb. "It helps," she agreed pleasantly. "But, lucky for me—and for all our Lombard Airways passengers—I'm not a flight attendant. I'm a flight instructor. Ted and Steve are two of my current crop of pupils. Hey, maybe I'll see you later? I have to run now. I promised to meet my other two pupils at a local beach for a swim. Bye!"

"Bye," Jillian echoed hollowly, absently raising a hand to waggle her fingers in a weak farewell in Nicky's direction, then allowed herself to collapse against the nearby wall once Nicky's apartment door was closed.

Ted's flight instructor? Jillian's mind was reeling. Ted had mentioned his instructors by name a couple of times, and she believed there might have been a "Nick" in there somewhere.

But she hadn't really been paying too much attention to names. All she had cared to hear was how well Ted was doing and how soon he'd actually begin his duties as a probationary copilot.

She closed her eyes and mentally reconstructed Nicky's face. How old could she be? Surely she'd have to be older than Ted, if she had already progressed to the position of flight instructor? "Well, if she is, she's damned well preserved!" Jillian concluded aloud, an uncharacteristic stab of jealousy stiffening her spine.

A second image, just as depressing, entered her mind—an image of Ted and Nicky alone together inside a flight simulator. How close were the quarters in the flight cabin of a commercial airplane, anyway?

All thoughts of an old-fashioned hearty breakfast for Ted, prepared by the hands of his loving wife, fled as Jillian pushed herself away from the wall and headed back up the stairs, intent on waking Ted and making his morning as rotten as hers was turning out to be!

Ted had awakened with the closing of the front door as Jillian had left the apartment. He blinked and sat up quickly, instantly alert and just as instantly lonely in the half empty bed.

"Now where in hell is she going at this hour?" he wondered out loud as he gathered clean clothes and made his way to the bathroom for a quick shower. He wasn't worried. She wouldn't get lost. After all, Jillian was a grown woman. She probably couldn't sleep and wanted to take a walk around the neighborhood rather than risk waking him up.

What a considerate wife he had. Considerate and loving and—he smiled as he stood under the needle-sharp spray of warm water—sexy as hell! The evening might have gotten off to a rocky start, but it had ended just as he'd dreamed it would all those long, lonely nights he'd been the only one in the queen-size bed.

Maybe even better!

He had dressed in slacks and a knit shirt, made his way into the kitchen for a cup of instant coffee he'd heated in the microwave and was just heading for the balcony to drink it when the door opened again and Jillian stepped inside the apartment.

"Mornin', Slugger," Ted said, quickly putting down the coffee cup and walking toward her, his arms held wide so that she could step into his embrace. The day outside was pleasant, but it was his wonderful, loving Jillian who really hung out the sun for him, and he could tell this was going to be one beautiful day.

He tried to gather her into his arms, intending to press a kiss on her cheek. "You weren't gone long. What's the matter? Were you afraid you'd get lost in the big city?"

She ducked down, neatly slipping out from under his arms, and walked over to the dining area. Carefully laying his keys on the table she turned to glare at him, her steely-eyed expression not doing a whole lot for his optimism about their plans for the day.

"I had originally planned to go to a nearby store and buy something for breakfast," she told him, something in her tone reminding him of the way his mother had spoken to his father whenever he had come home late and hadn't bothered to call first and tell her about the delay. "But then, before I could even go outside and get lost, I met one of your neighbors."

"Oh?" Ted replied with deliberate casualness, stepping over the raised back of the couch and reclining his long body on the cushions. *Oh, indeed,* he thought, racking his brain to figure out why Jillian seemed so distant, so rigid. *Am I supposed to know what's going on now, or is she going to say something else?*

"Her name is Nicky Hunter," Jillian continued at last, still standing next to the table, her hands clasped together in front of her. "She says she's one of your flight instructors."

Ted smiled, relaxing against the cushions. "Nick? Yeah, she's one of my slave drivers. Good, old Nick. One of the youngest in the business, and damn good at what she does. Did you meet her roommate?"

Jillian shook her head as if brushing aside his question and took three steps in his direction, her eyes narrowed. "Good old Nick? Oh, cut me a break! Ted, why didn't you tell me one of your instructors was a woman? A *beautiful* woman?"

He raised his eyebrows quizzically at the question, then shrugged his shoulders. "You didn't ask?" he returned, in what he hoped was in a loving, teasing way.

"Very funny, Ted. You're a real laugh riot."

Ted grimaced and sat up. Obviously, Jillian hadn't found anything amusing in his answer. As a matter of fact, Ted considered thoughtfully, if it were true that looks could kill, he would soon be in line for a starring role at the local funeral parlor.

Privately, he felt somewhat flattered that Jillian could believe she should be jealous about Nick's place in his life.

He was about to beg forgiveness, just as he supposed husbands in his position should do—even though he knew he hadn't done anything to beg forgiveness for—when another thought struck him. This wasn't some scene out of a television sitcom. Jillian was *really* upset!

That realization angered him. Sure, Nicky Hunter was an interesting, intelligent woman. And, hell—he would have had to have failed his last eye exam not to see that she was also one very beautiful woman. What of it? He was a happily married man, dammit! What right did Jillian have to start playing the role of jealous wife?

"Now, look, Slugger," he began, crossing the room to take hold of her arm. "I think you're overreacting here. What is it? Have you heard one too many lame jokes about what supposedly goes on in the flight cabin? Oh, and by the way, Nick's roommate's name is Todd. He's six-six, and plays football. Even love 'em and leave 'em Steve steers clear of Nick."

Jillian's angry glare faltered, then collapsed, leaving her looking faintly embarrassed. "Oh, Ted, I'm sorry," she said, turning into his arms. Her voice was muffled against his chest as she continued. "I don't know why I'm acting this way, honestly I don't."

Then, as quickly as she had capitulated, she seemed to rally, pushing clear of him. "Wait a minute! *Yes!* Yes, I do! I *do* know why I'm acting this way. I didn't really think anything is going on between you and Nicky. It's just that there's barely anything going on between you and *me!*"

She walked into the living room area and turned around in a full circle, then stopped and spread her arms wide, as if trying to encompass the room, the whole apartment, their entire marriage within the reach of her hands.

"This is crazy, Ted. This whole setup. You here and me back in Allentown. We're supposed to be married, Ted, and yet I barely see you. You have a whole life away from me and I have a whole life away from you. When are we supposed to begin building a life *together?*"

She pressed a hand against her forehead and turned her back to him, her slim shoulders slumped in what looked suspiciously like defeat.

Truly concerned, he approached Jillian without saying a word and pulled her around and into his arms, holding her tightly, as if she might disappear if he didn't.

"Oh, God, Ted—I hate this," he heard her announce against his shoulder, although her voice had lowered to little more than an injured whisper. "I mean, I thought I could be a grown-up about it, but I really, *really* hate this!"

Chapter Seven

Ted's arms were so strong, so solid, so wonderfully comforting, as he held her tightly against him, telling her everything was going to be fine if only they would be patient. She needed to hear him, to touch him. She craved this closeness, this assurance that he loved her.

He smelled of soap and shaving cream and the cologne she had given him—the same cologne he'd left a bottle of on the dresser in their bedroom in Allentown. The same cologne she sometimes opened and sniffed reminiscently, her eyes tightly closed in an attempt to conjure up his image, his love.

And she did love him. So much. So very much.

She loved him, Jillian thought ashamedly, and she was making his world a living hell with her childish outbursts, her idiotic jealousy, her totally unreasonable demands.

What was wrong with her? She was with her husband, she was in San Francisco, that beautiful city by the bay that had been immortalized in song and film. It was a glorious Saturday morning, and she had all of today and tomorrow and most of Monday to be alone with her husband.

So, why was she wasting her time feeling sorry for herself?

Slowly, as she allowed Ted's strength to soothe her, Jillian gathered her scattered emotions and forced them back under control.

Jillian began moving her arms so that she could slide them around his slim waist, the palms of her hands lightly pressing against the bare skin of his back.

She eased her body closer to his, melting against him.

She trailed feather-light kisses across his muscular shoulder and along the corded length of his throat.

She insinuated her thigh between his legs, pressing against him intimately.

"If you're trying to make up, Slugger," she heard him growl deep in his throat, "I think I'd better tell you something—it's working."

Suddenly her world, which had seemed so gray, so upside-down, a few minutes earlier, brightened and righted itself. Leaning back in his arms she looked up into his face, not caring that her cheeks were still damp with tears, not caring that she probably didn't look her best.

"I'm very glad to hear that, darling. The day it doesn't, I'll start worrying again. But for now, please forgive me for being such a spoiled brat. I don't know what came over me."

Ted leaned down, kissing her lightly on the mouth, then eased her toward the couch. Once seated side by side, his arm around her shoulders, he said, "I know what came over you. It's the same thing that comes over me sometimes, when I wake up at three o'clock in the morning for no reason and you're not there."

Jillian nodded, knowing her tears were still not that well buried. "And," she added, "when I come home after a long day at the playground with the kids and wish we could have supper and then sit out on the back steps and talk over our day while we both unwind."

He pulled her close to his chest so that she could rest her head against him, and said, "And when I think I'm never going to get out of that damn flight simulator for good and I need you here to tell me I'm terrific. And when I wonder why we're doing this to each other and want to call it quits and come home. And when I see couples walking hand in hand toward the ocean as the sun is beginning to set and I'm so lonely for you that I can taste it. And when—"

Jillian, suddenly happy again, snuggled even closer, peered up at him playfully and interrupted, saying, "And when your clothes hamper is overflowing and your refrigerator is empty and all your dishes are dirty?"

He looked down at her, mischief dancing in his clear blue eyes. "Yeah, well, maybe then, too. Just the way you miss me when the faucets leak or your car makes funny noises or there's a sudden thunderstorm. When that storm came up last time I was home, I thought you were going to crawl under the dining room table."

"I was not!" Jillian gave him a playful punch in the belly and sat up straight. Did he have to bring that up? She might like to consider herself a competent adult, but thunderstorms still held the power to turn her into a quivering mass of nerves.

"Really? I'll remember that next time there's a storm and you come running to me for protection."

"Okay, okay. I admit it. I love you madly, Ted Hackett, but there are times when it's just plain nice to have somebody else in the house. It might not be that big a place, but it can sure feel that way when I'm all alone. I was alone before, when Mother left for Spain, but it's different now somehow. Lonelier. I don't know why. Maybe I ought to buy a dog or something."

"A dog? Are you saying that you think you can replace me with a wet nose, four legs and a wagging tail? Thanks a heap!"

"Think nothing of it. But don't worry, darling—I won't name him Theodore. And I won't let him have any of your biscuits."

Ted smiled, then just as quickly sobered. "You know, Slugger, you and I aren't the only ones going through this commuter-marriage business. I've met three other guys out here who are doing the same thing, one of them for six months and the others for over a year. And they don't have just wives in another city, they have families—their kids—living almost half a country away from them."

Jillian nodded. "I know," she said, grudgingly admitting that she, too, had been thinking about the subject as it pertained to couples other than themselves. "Sometimes at the airport I see servicemen coming back from overseas. The reunions always make me cry, even more now than they did before we were married. I don't know how those families do it, with either the mommy or the daddy away for months, maybe even a year at a time."

"At least we see each other twice a month," Ted said, rising to pick up his now cold cup of coffee and carry it into the kitchen. "And it's not just service families, either. In today's economy a person has to go where the job takes him or her, and sometimes that means leaving a family behind until it's possible for them to be together again."

She followed after him, taking the cup and rinsing it in the sink before preparing another cupful for him. "I didn't tell you this before, darling, but I've been reading up on the subject. Marriages like ours are becoming more common in America every day. I read in one article that six percent of all married couples live in separate cities—double that of ten years ago. Six percent may not sound like many—but it translates to one and a half million couples. Those couples are doing it—so why can't we?"

Ted levered himself up onto the countertop, his long, tanned legs dangling a few inches above the floor, and peered at her quizzically. "Is that what's wrong, Slugger? You've been reading about families that are coping and wondering why you and I can't seem to get with the program?"

Jillian pushed a hand through her hair, pulling a face. "You don't have to be so blunt about it, Ted," she said, bristling slightly. "But, yes, that is one thing that's bothering me. You seem to be doing fine, but if everyone else can do it... why am *I* having so much trouble? And it's not as if we're the only ones to have this happen to them within days of the honeymoon. Think of all the couples that get married shortly before one of them ships out with the navy or something like that. Mom and Dad were married only a few months before he left for Vietnam.

"Of course," she ended quietly, "Dad never came back."

The thought of the father she had never known and the old, battered recliner in the corner of her living room, the chair that Ted had taken for his own after it had not been sat in for so many years, momentarily saddened her. She determinedly turned away from both Ted and the unhappy memory, slipping the coffee cup into the microwave and hitting the reheat button.

Why was she beating around the bush? It was time she said exactly what was on her mind, what she thought about late at night when she stayed downstairs watching television rather than climb the steps to her lonely bedroom.

She took a deep breath, turned to face him and said, "Or maybe we're not coping very well because we're doing it for the wrong reasons. We're not serving our country, Ted. My father *had* to go. We don't *have* to do this. We're doing this strictly for economic reasons. Maybe even for selfish reasons."

Ted hopped down from the countertop, his scowl telling her of his anger even before he spoke. "Aren't you forgetting something, Jill? You have a contract with Baird's. You've committed to them for two years. And even if you could get out of the contract somehow, this position is something you've been longing for ever since you got your teaching degree. Or am I wrong and you like being a substitute teacher, not ever knowing exactly when you'd be working, not being able to really get to know your pupils, to really sink your teeth into your job?"

The buzzer went off on the microwave and Jill motioned to the appliance with a wave of her hand, letting Ted know that if he wanted to drink coffee at a time like this, then he could darn well just get it himself.

"No, I haven't forgotten," she said, folding her arms at her waist, a move she knew looked defensive, but she didn't care. She had been on a roller coaster ever since her plane had touched down in San Francisco and she was becoming pretty frustrated by the feeling. "I'm not saying that I *want* to give up my position at Baird's. I'm just wondering if I'm not being selfish keeping it, when my husband is three thousand miles away."

Ted's left eyebrow rose a fraction, a trick he had of expressing himself without words that usually intrigued her, even excited her—although at the moment she felt more like hitting him than kissing him. "Ah, I get it now. You're feeling *guilty.*"

"No I am *not!*" Jillian exploded quickly, then added honestly, "Oh, all right—yes. Yes, I am. I don't know why, but I am."

"I do, Slugger. You're feeling guilty because you want a career of your own. Guilty because your husband is on one coast while you're on the other. Guilty because you aren't here to take care of me the way your mother took care of you or the way she pulled up stakes without a blink to follow your stepfather to Barcelona."

"Maybe," Jillian answered quietly, knowing that he had struck a nerve. She *was* old-fashioned. She'd be the first to admit it—although she didn't much like having Ted point it out for her. She firmly believed that a woman's place was at her husband's side.

And what was so wrong with that idea, anyway? That sort of arrangement had worked since the beginning of time.

It was traditional, wasn't it?

Ted took a single step in her direction, so that she backed up a pace into the dining area. "It bothers you that you aren't here to take care of me, to cook for me, to clean for me, to make sure my socks match when I leave in the morning."

He took another step forward and Jillian retreated all the way into the living room. "And what's so very wrong with that?" she questioned him, her eyes narrowing. "You're my husband, Ted—not my playmate. And it's not just that I want to play house or something. We're *married*. I'm *supposed* to make sure your socks match!"

He shook his head. "No, you're not. I've been matching my own socks for years now. I didn't marry you to gain a mother or a housekeeper, or even because I adore making love with you. I married you, Jillian Hackett, because I couldn't imagine my life without you. *You* are my family, *you* are my life, and we can make up our own rules to suit us—not to suit some sort of outmoded notion of what's right or wrong for families. I don't want you to throw away the career you're trying to build, your love of teaching, just so you can greet me with my pipe and slippers when I come through the door at night."

"You don't smoke a pipe," Jillian pointed out quietly, although she was beginning to feel a comfortable warmth invade her chest. Ted was being masterful, and although she considered herself fairly liberated she rather liked the feeling.

"Don't interrupt, Slugger," he said, his smile in evidence once more, "at least not when I'm just getting on a roll. I didn't tell you about Nick Hunter because to me she's just a good teacher. Okay, so she's beautiful. I'm married, not dead. I know when a woman is beautiful. But I don't want Nick. I want *you*. I love *you*. I want us to be together. And we will be together—either here or in Allentown or in Timbuktu—but we *will* be together. We're going to make it through this, Slugger, I promise. It won't be easy, but we're going to make it."

He stopped in front of her, lightly squeezing her upper arms in his hands. "One way or the other, we're going to make it!"

"Oh, Ted," Jillian said, throwing her arms around his neck. "Hold me! Hold me and love me and make me feel married!"

His smile nearly made her toes curl in her sneakers. "Okay, Slugger. First I'll take you into the bedroom, kiss you senseless and make mad, passionate love to you, and then I'll make you sort all the dirty laundry I've got stuffed in my bottom drawer."

Jillian wrinkled her nose at the last part of his statement. "I said I wanted to feel like a married woman, darling—not your personal maid. Or is that really why you invited me out here? To clean up after you?"

"Not on your life, lady," he said, slipping his arms around her and lifting her high against his chest as he headed for the bedroom.

His lips met hers in a searing kiss just as they entered the bedroom, and somewhere in the back of her mind Jillian realized that several months after the fact she had finally been carried over the threshold.

Ted awoke, startled, surprised to realize he had fallen asleep, even though he knew he hadn't slept very much since Jillian had arrived on Friday.

Not that I'm complaining or anything, he told himself, smiling ruefully as he turned over onto his stomach on the blanket and looked down at his wife, who was still sound asleep, the late Monday afternoon sun turning her hair to soft, warm copper.

His gaze left her face and traveled down over the length of her body. The white two-piece bathing suit couldn't be called a bikini—at least not by California standards—but it concealed and revealed in all the right places.

Jillian's body was a symphony of classic perfection, her legs long and straight, her hips slightly flaring, her stomach smooth and concave beneath the swell of her breasts.

He knew every inch of her, had kissed, caressed and worshiped every satiny portion, from her flat, shell-like ears to her slim insteps. He knew her body better than he knew his own.

Yet did he really know this woman? Did he really know Jillian Hackett, his bride, his wife? He propped himself up on his elbows and stared out at the waves breaking against the sand.

He and Jillian had met and married within the space of a few months. There had been no real reason to delay the marriage, not with her mother overseas and unable to fly home for the wedding and his own parents dead, his remaining relatives scattered all over the country, from Florida to Alaska.

Besides, he had wanted Jillian for his wife the first time he had seen her at the health club, walking along with such confident strides, her head held high, a smile for everyone she met. It had taken him two weeks, but he had finally engineered his meeting with her on the racquetball court.

From the very beginning it had seemed as if she had stepped out of his fantasies and into reality, the woman with whom he would share his life, his dreams. The woman who would be the mother to his children, the mate who would grow old with him while keeping him forever young.

What was the use in dragging the thing out once she realized what he had already known—that they had been made for each other?

They hadn't rushed blindly into this marriage, however. They had sat down together and seriously discussed their hopes, their dreams. Jillian knew he would eventually have to move to the coast for training in order to become a first officer. She had planned to go with him, although they had agreed that he would choose Allentown for his permanent assignment when it became possible.

She also had known that his job would sometimes keep him away from home for days at a time, whenever he was scheduled for long flights. She had accepted that, just as she had been pleasantly surprised to learn that there would be times when he would be home for nearly a week at a time, between flights.

They had spoken of her summer vacations, between school terms, and the short trips they could take when he had extended layovers in Allentown.

It had all seemed so simple—until they had returned from their honeymoon to learn that his promotion had come earlier than expected.

So simple—until he had been forced to leave Allentown and Jillian behind in order to advance his career.

So very, very simple—until she hadn't been able to secure a teaching position in San Francisco and they'd had to settle for this mutually unattractive commuter marriage—this marriage in a suitcase— with neither of them settled, with neither of them feeling all that "married."

Maybe their argument Saturday morning had been a good thing. Maybe it had cleared the air. They certainly hadn't had any problems since then, thank goodness—spending the remainder of the weekend seeing the sights and sleeping in each other's arms after long hours of loving.

But now it was Monday afternoon, and after a day on the beach, laughing and playing in the ocean, it was nearly time to pack up and head back to the apartment before driving Jillian to the airport.

Ted's gut clenched at the thought of watching her walk through the gate that would lead her to the airplane, taking her away from him again for God only knew how long.

He would be flying, actually having some hands-on experience, for the next three weeks, and he didn't know if he'd be able to make it back to Allentown until the very end of the month—not that he had told Jillian that yet.

He had planned to tell her, had wanted to—but the timing for such an announcement hadn't been right for the whole weekend. She had been so happy, so magnificent, that he hadn't had the heart to say anything about it—especially since Nick would be flying with him. Ted didn't honestly believe that Jillian was still jealous of Nick, but he also knew that the information might serve to hurt his wife's feelings.

And the last thing he wanted was to hurt Jillian. "Slugger?"

"Hmm?" Jillian murmured beside him, her eyes fluttering open, only to quickly close again when she looked directly into the sun. Shielding her eyes with her hand, she rolled onto her side and looked up at

him. "Ted? Did I fall asleep? I've never fallen asleep on a beach before! It's a good thing we used my sunblock cream, or we'd both be burned to a crisp. What time is it?"

He smiled down at her, noticing the way her hip curved and dipped toward her small waist. "Time for Cinderella to leave the ball, I'm afraid," he said, then gave in to temptation and rolled her onto her back once more, to feed hungrily on her moist, pink mouth as she slid her arms around him, pulling him close.

She tasted like sunshine and saltwater, and he never wanted to let her go.

But he hadn't been kidding—it was time to leave. They had a little less than four hours before her flight. Slowly, reluctantly, he released her, and together they began gathering up their belongings before heading for a nearby parking lot and Steve Hammond's car.

Once back in the apartment they showered together, washing the sand from their bodies and hair, then made a brief, delightful detour to the bed before rushing into their clothing and heading for the airport, Jillian suddenly worried that she might miss her flight and not get home in time to prepare for her first day of school.

"As it is, I bet I'll be the only teacher there copiously yawning into my study plan," she said, snuggling against him in the front seat of the car. "Thank goodness the students only have a half day tomorrow and no real classes. If I don't fall asleep during the afternoon faculty meeting I just might not lose my job."

Ted pulled the car into the Lombard Airways lot, switched off the ignition and smiled at his wife. "Are you by chance insinuating that I've kept you from your bed all weekend?"

"Nope," she answered, kissing his cheek before moving away to grab her purse. "I'm insinuating that you've kept me *in* bed for most of this glorious weekend. You just didn't let me get much sleep in that bed. How am I ever going to face a classroom of innocent second-graders when I've just spent such a deliciously decadent weekend?"

"With a big smile?" Ted suggested as he helped her from the car, his own grin wide and faintly wicked, before his mood changed without warning and he became serious. "More important, Slugger—how am I going to face that apartment tonight without you?"

Quick tears sparkled in her eyes, her beautiful, expressive eyes that looked so very green against the golden tan she had added to during their weekend in the sun. "Probably the same way I face the house when I come back from driving you to the airport. Badly. Very badly."

Ted frowned at her words. He had never thought about that before—about what it was like to be the one left behind, rather than the one who did the leaving. "God, Slugger, I'm sorry. I didn't think—I never realized..."

Her smile was sad, but her words were sadder still. "I understand, darling. You hadn't thought about what it has been like for me to come back to a silent, empty house and still feel your presence—to see a shirt you left behind in the hamper, your recliner chair sitting there, empty. You didn't realize what it was like to turn on the stereo and hear your favorite compact disc begin to play."

She sighed, looking at him sadly. "And you didn't have to think about what it has been like for me to crawl into an empty bed and smell your after-shave on the sheets. I didn't know either—until you left for the first time."

Those words lingered in his mind after he had kissed her goodbye.

They replayed in his head long after he had watched her plane rise into the sky, taking her away from him...

...long after he had gone back to his empty apartment to discover that she had forgotten one of her headbands on the dining room table...

...long after he had eaten a solitary dinner and wished Steve would come back soon so the apartment wouldn't feel so damn empty.

But the memory of her words was loudest and hurt most as he crawled into his lonely bed sometime after midnight and buried his head in her pillow, breathing in lingering traces of Jillian's perfume.

Chapter Eight

"You *fought* with him? With *Ted?* Why? What did he do—leave the top off the toothpaste? I mean, the two of you aren't married long enough to have any sort of real fight."

Jillian pressed her fingers to either side of her head, slowly massaging her throbbing temples. She had just finished picking at a tuna-fish sandwich she hadn't really wanted in the first place, when Barbara had knocked on the back door and come inside. And just as it had always been, they sat at Jillian's kitchen table, having a heart-to-heart chat.

It was silly really, but even as Jillian felt grateful for her friend's company she also felt a bit depressed by it. Jillian just believed *something* should have changed now that she was a married woman—even if it was only that this house would seem more like Ted's and hers, rather than a never-changing leftover from her childhood.

"It was just a little argument," Jillian explained as her friend sat down across the table from her. "Besides, we made up again a few minutes later."

A reminiscent smile curled the edges of her mouth and her green eyes became dreamy as she remembered lying in Ted's arms, making love for most of each night. "Boy, did we make up again."

Barbara leaned forward, grinning. "Details, Jill. I *demand* details—the juicier the better."

"Barb! I can't do that!" Jillian's smile faded abruptly as she realized she shouldn't have said anything about the argument that had taken place six days ago in San Francisco. And she most certainly shouldn't have said anything about how she and Ted had made up after that argument.

Some things were, well, some things were *private,* that's all.

"We're not in high school any more, Barb," she continued in explanation, hurriedly picking up her sandwich plate and going to the sink. "It's just—well, it's just too personal."

"Too personal, huh? You mean like the time I told you about Bobby Yeager and where we went after the senior prom? Or maybe you mean the time you cried all over me when Joe Peterson ditched you for that cheerleader your junior year of college? Or maybe those times weren't really *personal.*"

"Ouch!" Jillian responded quickly, recognizing the disillusionment and pain in her friend's voice. "Boy, Barb, when you're right, you're right. Of course those things were personal. They were our deepest secrets—at the time. But it's different now. Ted isn't my latest boyfriend. He's my *husband.*"

"And you've got a point, Jill. You're married now. You and Ted will be getting a house of your own one of these days. Pretty soon after that you'll be having babies. We won't have anything in common. Oh, you'll telephone once in a while and I'll visit you and Ted Junior in your four-bedroom colonial in the suburbs, but it won't be the same."

"Come on, Barb. Aren't you getting a little carried away?" Jillian scoffed. "We'll always be friends. You know that."

But Barb kept talking, as if she hadn't heard a word. "Gee, we played together in the same playpen. We started kindergarten together, double-dated when we were fifteen, graduated from the same college. And now it's over. Finished. *Kaput!*"

Barbara took a long drink of lemonade and then she grinned. "Are you feeling sorry for me yet, Jilly? I mean, this is an Oscar-worthy performance, you know. You should be at least feeling misty-eyed at your poor old childhood chum's woe."

Jillian relaxed and pulled a tissue from her pocket, to dramatically wipe at her dry eyes. "Is this good enough, Barb? What can I do to make it 'all better' for you? Do you want a cookie? But, seriously, do you really think I have been avoiding you or something?" Barb might have been teasing her, but Jillian detected a hint of truth in all she'd said—and even felt a little guilty.

Barbara shook her head, although she avoided Jillian's eyes as she said, "No, Jilly. Don't feel guilty. You're married now and things have to change. If they didn't, something would be wrong. So, hey—just forget I said anything in the first place. Honestly—everything's fine."

Only everything wasn't fine and Jillian knew it. She reached across the table and took Barbara's hands in her own. "Barb, I'm sorry about Labor Day weekend. It was rotten of me to change our plans at the last minute like that. And I'm sorry that I haven't seen much of you this week. But I've really been busy, settling in at Baird. It's only Thursday, and I'm already snowed under with work. My professors warned me that schoolteachers don't really get done with their work when the three o'clock bell rings, but I had no idea I'd have to bring so much home with me at night. Between keeping house, working on lesson plans, and talking with Ted on the phone, I—"

"I know," Barbara answered sincerely, squeezing Jillian's hands before releasing them. Then she wrinkled her nose in an exaggerated grimace of distaste. "Did I tell you that my mom kept me busy all three days of the holiday weekend? As soon as she heard you were going to San Francisco and the picnic was canceled she wrote down a list of chores as long as my arm—while you came back from California with a tan!"

Jillian laughed out loud. "No wonder you're mad at me! Look, Barb—let me make it up to you, okay? Ted won't be home for another three weeks, so the entire weekend is mine. Correction—the entire weekend is *yours!* Name your poison. What do you want to do?"

"No kidding?" Barbara asked. Her smile was so grateful that Jillian longed to kick herself for not realizing sooner that Barbara had to feel as if she were only good enough when Ted wasn't around—and that she, Jillian, had dropped her best friend like a hot rock the moment Ted had appeared on her personal horizon.

"No kidding," Jillian repeated, then added as had been their custom ever since childhood, "cross my heart and hope to spit!"

Ted took a taxi in from the airport, not wanting to spoil his surprise. By some unbelievable stroke of luck, he had been given the weekend off, and he had grabbed the jump seat on the last flight in from the coast, arriving a little after eleven.

He supposed that Jillian wasn't asleep yet, still waiting up for his usual telephone call—and probably pretty angry at that, because he had told her he'd phone at eight o'clock, Eastern Daylight Time.

Only he hadn't, because he'd known that if he did he would have given the game away, and he wanted to see the look of delighted surprise on Jillian's beautiful face when he slipped his key into the lock and opened the front door.

Had it only been five days since he'd seen Jillian off on her own plane? It seemed more like five years, even if his training had kept him pretty busy. The days went by quickly enough—it was just the nights that got to him.

Boy, did the nights get to him. Steve was barely in the apartment, having found a neighborhood restaurant and bar that provided a happy-hour buffet he swore was not only a great place to eat but also a great place to "meet"—to meet women, of course.

And what of it? Steve was a carefree bachelor. He didn't have any strings tying him to someone who was three thousand miles away. Although even if he did, Ted had gotten the impression that having a wife or girlfriend back in Texas wouldn't slow Steve down for long.

Ted relaxed against the cracked leather seat of the taxi cab, smiling ruefully when he remembered his one and only excursion to the restaurant with Steve and two other pilots.

He had spent half the evening bending some nubile Lombard Airways flight attendant's ear about Jillian, probably boring the woman out of her mind, and the rest of the evening sitting alone in a corner wondering how a nice guy like him had ended up in such a place.

He probably ought to join a health club or something, to help him work off his excess energy—and frustration—but he wanted to save every penny he could. Both he and Jillian had let their memberships lapse in the club they had belonged to in Allentown for just that reason.

Every spare dollar, every extra penny they could squeeze until it yelled for mercy, had been earmarked for their future.

And so far they had been doing fairly well. As a matter of fact, if they could keep to their budget, Jillian might be able to join him at the end of the school year, after all—whether she could secure another teaching position in San Francisco or not.

Why, even this unexpected trip home would be cost effective, Ted decided, knowing he was stretching the point. But two could eat at home cheaper than one of them—namely him—could eat out.

Oh, who was he kidding? He hadn't flown to Allentown for an inexpensive meal. He had been willing to ride in the baggage compartment—even strap himself on top of the plane and flap his arms all the way across country—to see Jillian, to hold her, to kiss her, to tell her that his apartment had never seemed so empty as it had since she had walked out of it on Monday, leaving behind a thousand small memories that haunted him morning and night.

The cab pulled to a screeching halt at the curb, shaking him out of his thoughts. He paid the fare, picked up his small flight bag and stepped out onto the pavement, looking up the walkway at the neatly edged petunia beds that were illuminated by the yellow porch light as well as a spill of light from the living room windows.

He mounted the steps to the front door two at a time, hunting in his pocket for his key. He rang the doorbell twice in quick succession, then let himself into the small foyer.

"Jill?" he called out, slightly bewildered that she hadn't already come running to see who was at the door. "Slugger? Where the heck are you?"

He looked into the small living room, noticing that while two table lamps were lit both the television and stereo were switched off. Frowning in confusion, he made his way through the downstairs, then climbed the stairs, still calling Jillian's name.

Nothing.

The house was completely empty.

"Where in hell—" he wondered out loud, reentering the kitchen and opening the refrigerator, to help himself to a can of iced tea.

There wasn't a single can of iced tea in the refrigerator or any to be found in the cabinet.

"And why should there be?" he asked himself rhetorically as he took out a can of soda and shut the cabinet door firmly, knowing Jillian hadn't expected him home for another three weeks.

But not having any iced tea in the house was one thing. Not having Jillian in the house was another. Where would she have gone, knowing that he would be calling?

Calling. Of course. Why didn't I think of that before? Ted snapped his fingers and headed into the dining room, to push the outgoing message button on Jillian's answering machine.

"Hello," he heard Jillian's voice say. "I'm not home at the moment, but if you will leave your name and a short message and the time of your call at the beep, I'll get back to you as soon as possible. And Ted, if that's you—I'm out with Barb, darling. I'll call you the moment I get home, honest!"

Out with Barb? *Oh, really,* Ted thought nastily, taking a swig of soda, then grimacing as he realized he had picked up a can of diet soda. He hated diet soda. *And just where would Jillian and Barbara—the very single, unattached Barbara—go on a Friday night that would keep them out until,* he looked down at his watch, *until damn near midnight?*

"Hackett, you're losing it!" he announced out loud in the quiet house as he went into the living room and collapsed into the recliner chair. "Jill's no more guilty of doing anything wrong than you were the night you went out with Steve."

The thought soothed him, but he realized that he now knew a little bit of how Jillian had felt when she'd met Nick and discovered that one of his flight instructors was a young, beautiful woman.

"Jealousy is a two-way street, Hackett," he said, reaching for the remote control and turning on the television, resigned to wait impatiently until Jillian came home and equally resigned to the knowledge that his plan to surprise his wife had backfired, leaving him alone with an unappetizing can of diet soda and a bad 1950s-era cowboy movie.

The good guys had just come riding over the hill to rescue the innocent rancher from the gang of dirty, low-down cattle rustlers when Ted heard Jill's key in the back door. He looked at his watch—for the third time in as many minutes—to see that it was almost one-thirty.

He heard her lay her keys on the kitchen table, and sat quietly as she walked into the living room, knowing she could hear the television.

He didn't know why he continued to keep silent, sure that she must be wondering if a robber had broken into the house, stolen all the family silver, then stopped to watch John Wayne play the hero, but he wasn't in the mood to stand up, spread his arms wide and yell, "Surprise!"

"Who's there?" Jillian called out, her voice slightly tremulous.

"It's me," Ted said on a sigh, wondering how low he could sink, to deliberately frighten his own wife. "Come on in and join the party. I think the hero is about to kiss his horse and then ride off into the sunset."

"Ted?" Jillian raced into the room, to stand between him and the television set. She was wearing her blue dress—one of his favorites. And she looked good enough to eat.

"Why? What?" Her confused frown disappeared, to be replaced by a glorious smile as he stood up and she threw herself into his arms. "Oh, darling—when did you get home? Why didn't you tell me?"

He stopped her question with his mouth, kissing her hungrily, then holding her close as the heady scent of her perfume teased his nostrils.

"I wanted to surprise you," he murmured into her hair before holding her away from him at arm's length. "Only you weren't here to be surprised. I got home at around eleven-thirty or so and listened to your tape on the answering machine. So—did you and Barb go to a movie?"

She put her hands to his cheeks, as if to assure herself that he really was here with her. "Dinner and a movie, and then to one of our favorite old college haunts for double-dip chocolate fudge sundaes, as a matter of fact. It was a positively decadent evening!" she said airily, leading him to the couch so that they could sit close together, her head on his shoulder.

"Oh, darling," she continued, "I'm so sorry I wasn't here. I left that message on the answering machine in case you called, knowing that with the three-hour time difference I'd be able to telephone you before you went to bed. But now you're here and I don't have to call at all. Wait until I tell Barb that you're—whoops!"

Ted felt Jillian stiffen in his arms. "Whoops, what? What's the matter, Slugger?"

She sat forward, her shoulders slumped, avoiding his eyes. "It's Barb, Ted. I felt so bad about canceling our Labor Day plans I promised her I'd do anything she wanted this weekend. The movies tonight, an antique show at the fairgrounds tomorrow afternoon and dinner and ice skating at the new indoor rink tomorrow night. And then on Sunday I'm supposed to man one of the tables at the school's annual bake sale."

Ted could tell from Jillian's tone that she was serious, although he couldn't see the problem. To him, the solutions were simple. "So? Get one of the other teachers to sit in at the bake sale in exchange for helping her out some other time. Go to the antique show if you want to, as I suppose it's only open tomorrow. I'm a big boy now, and I'm sure I can find something to do while you're gone. Barb will understand if you cancel out on the rest of the day."

"Oh, yeah, right. Sure she will," Jillian answered dully. "That's easy for you to say. Just the way she 'understood' how I canceled our plans when I had a chance to fly to San Francisco to be with you. Oh, brother. Barb's right. I do use her for company whenever I'm lonely, then drop her like a hot potato whenever you're in town."

Ted scratched his head, wondering why women always made such a big deal out of things. "I think you've lost me. Let me get this straight, Slugger," he said, pulling her back against him. "It's not bad enough that we've been married since June and have only been able to see each other every couple of weeks since then? Now we have to apologize to *Barb* for wanting to be together when we can?"

Jillian twisted in his arms, looking up at him wistfully. "It does sound sort of crazy when you say it that way," she admitted. "But it's not just Barb. You and I might be married, but our lives are so separate that when we do have a chance to spend some extra time together, I just want to drop everything. Yet part of me feels it's just not right. But I can't just hang around the house all weekend, without *any* plans because you might—by some miracle—show up. I guess I'm left with the choice of being unfair to myself, or unfair to other people. I know that sounds pretty garbled, darling. Am I making myself clear?"

"As crystal, unfortunately, which, I have to admit, kinda scares me. Dammit, Slugger, I'm beginning to feel like I didn't do anybody any favors by showing up around here tonight," Ted grumbled, slowly shaking his head.

"Idiot! That's not what I'm talking about at all! I can't tell you how happy I am that you were able to come home for the weekend, and I'm sure I can get Margaret Simms to substitute for me on Sunday. I took her entire class of hellions on a field trip to the game preserve this week when she came down with a cold, so she owes me one." Jillian laid her hands on his shoulders and leaned forward to kiss him lingeringly on the mouth, her body pressed invitingly against his, and he drew her fully into his arms, eagerly returning her kiss.

It might have been well after one o'clock in the morning in Allentown, but Ted's body was still merrily ticking along on West Coast time, and he was more than ready to adjourn to the second floor and continue what Jillian had seemed so willing to begin.

He had just eased away from her slightly in preparation of suggesting just such a move when she said, "You know, darling, it's just like I read in that magazine article I told you about last weekend. Commuter couples—that's us—have a lot of problems other couples don't have. One of them that I didn't really think about before is that they tend to allow their friendships to falter because they're intent on keeping their weekends free for their mates."

Ted lifted the fall of hair from Jillian's shoulder and began nuzzling her throat. "And another problem is that when they do get together, one of them wants to talk while the other wants to get on to more important modes of communication."

She tilted her head to one side, to allow him easier access to the perfumed curve of her neck. "Now you're being silly," she admonished, giggling when he blew his warm breath gently into her ear, an action which he knew always sent shivers racing down her spine. He knew it because Jill, bless her, was a vocal lover, free with her affection and lavish with her praise. She was a wonder, a constant delight.

And he wanted her so much right now that he could barely see straight.

Ted reached behind her to begin unzipping her dress. *Progress.* He was definitely making progress! "Silly, you say? Now I know we have to do something about seeing each other more often, woman, if you can't tell the difference between when I'm joking and when I'm trying my damnedest to seduce my sexy wife."

He pulled her unceremoniously to her feet. "Therefore, I suggest we immediately adjourn to the bedroom for a hands-on lesson in nonverbal modes of communication." He leered at her playfully. "What do you think?"

"Sounds fascinating—especially the hands-on part," she said, dancing away from him and heading for the staircase in the dining room, not stopping until she had a hand on the newel post and one foot on the bottom step.

She winked at him, then slowly slid her skirt halfway up her silky thighs as she began to climb the stairs two at a time. "Race you to the bedroom!"

Ted hesitated only long enough to turn off the television set just as the credits were rolling up the screen, then headed upstairs, intent on making the most of this second chance to get their weekend off to a rousing beginning.

Chapter Nine

"Would you believe that the divorce rate for commuter marriages—I think I already told you that that's what our sort of marriage is called by the experts, didn't I—is about forty percent lower than that of the rest of married couples?"

"Those poor 'rest of married couples.' My heart bleeds for them." Ted turned his head on the pillow, looking at Jillian owlishly.

They had made love not fifteen minutes ago, and he was still basking in the warm afterglow, feeling good about himself, feeling good about Jillian, feeling pretty at peace with the whole world, as a matter of fact. It was nearly eleven o'clock in the morning, and the sun was streaming into the master bedroom through a slight chink in the ivory lace draperies.

"Oh, shut up. I'm not kidding. I *read* it—in a very reliable magazine article."

"Is that right, Dr. Hackett?" he asked, slipping his arm under the cotton sheet and across her waist. "I'm impressed. Truly, I am. And do you have any theories as to why us commuter-marriage types have racked up such impressive numbers?"

She snuggled closer to him, so that her hair brushed against his bare shoulder. "We try harder," she answered simply, running her fingers lightly over the fine mat of hair on his chest. "At least that's what I read in the article. We know the cards are stacked against us, so we go out of our way to make sure we don't fail. It makes sense in some twisted sort of way, I suppose."

Ted lifted her hand to his lips, kissing her fingertips. "I suppose. It also could be because we commuter-marriage-type men have the good sense to marry intelligent women like you who know that we won't have to live this way forever and the end result justifies the temporary inconvenience."

"Inconvenience?" Jillian turned onto her side, propping her chin in her hands. "Is that what you call it when I go into the bathroom in the morning and there's a spider in the bathtub big enough to have his own zip code—and my fearless bug-slaying husband is a full three thousand miles away, flying the friendly skies with Snow White? You call that an *inconvenience?*"

"Hey! I don't fly the friendly skies—I *soar* with Lombard Airways. And who the hell is Snow White? Don't tell me you mean *Nick?*"

"No," Jillian responded, rolling her eyes in mock disbelief. "I mean Steve. But never mind. I was trying to make a point here somewhere."

"Sorry for the interruption." Ted reached out and knocked one of her supporting elbows aside, so that she crashed ignominiously onto his chest.

Then he snaked his hand lower, gently cupping one firm breast. "Far be it from me to make you lose your train of thought," he said as he began lightly rubbing at her nipple with the pad of his thumb. He allowed his other hand to begin drawing slow, lazy circles at the base of her spine. "Please, Mrs. Hackett—continue your dissertation."

She covered his hand with her own, sliding it away from her breast and back into neutral territory. "You aren't going to be serious, are you, Ted?"

He rolled her over onto her back and followed after her, to begin nibbling at her earlobe. "What gave you that idea, Slugger?"

"You're more incorrigible than any of my second-graders—and that includes Jason Carruthers, who hid a huge, ugly frog in my desk yesterday!" But she grinned as she said it, and he knew he had won. There was a time and a place for serious discussion, but Ted didn't think that this morning had so far provided either of those things.

"Oh, you poor baby," he teased, lowering his mouth to within an inch of hers, captivated by her soft, pink lips. "And what did you do? Throw a saddle over that nasty old frog and ride it to the lunch room?"

Jillian slipped her hands up and over his bare shoulders. "Oh, very funny. Now why don't you just shut up and come here?"

He was just about to oblige when the telephone on the nightstand rang, interrupting what had so far borne all the earmarks of what could prove to be an interesting interlude. "Damn!" he exploded as Jillian turned to reach for the receiver. "Let it ring. Pretend you didn't hear it. Turn off the ringer. Better yet—I'll throw the whole telephone out the window."

She shook her head, pushing him away as she sat up, dragging the sheet up over her bare breasts. "Omigosh! We can't, Ted. It's probably Barb. Remember? I promised to go to the antique show with her this afternoon."

Ted fell back onto the mattress and covered his eyes with his forearm, the mood broken as if someone had just poured a pitcher of water over his head. Maybe two pitchers, both of them full of freezing cold ice water.

"How could I forget? Go ahead, Slugger, you'd better answer it. I'll be all right. I'll just lie here, a broken man—whimpering."

"Nut," Jillian said, laughing, then picked up the receiver. "Hello? Barb! I was just going to call you. What? *Of course* I haven't forgotten! I'll be ready in half an hour and meet you out back. Yes, of course. We'll grab a bite to eat on the way. Bye, now—I still have to jump in the shower."

She replaced the receiver with a sigh, then quickly pulled the top sheet entirely from the bed, wrapping its flowered length around herself as she made her way toward the hall bathroom, leaving her naked— and entirely unashamed—husband lying exposed on the mattress.

Stopping at the doorway, she turned to Ted, who was slowly reaching down beside the bed for the pair of shorts that had been discarded there earlier.

"There's some sandwich fixings in the refrigerator, darling," she told him, "and fresh rye bread in the bread box on the counter. You don't mind making your own lunch today, do you? And what are you going to do this afternoon, darling? Wash the car?"

He tugged on the shorts, zipping them with a flourish. "Yeah, I'll probably wash the car. *Both* of the cars. That's why I was in such a rush to get home—so I could wash the cars."

"Ted!" Jillian looked as if she might cry. "We have already discussed all of this. I'll tell Barb that you've come home and she'll understand that I have to cancel our plans for this evening. But I can't back out on the antique show, too. It just wouldn't be fair."

Ted sniffed, shaking his head and laughing hollowly at his, he knew, childish reaction to having *his* plans for the weekend rearranged. *But they had been such good plans!*

"I'm sorry, Slugger," he apologized, taking one long, last look at her as she stood there, her copper hair adorably mussed, one creamy bare shoulder rising above the togalike wrap of the sheet. "You and Barb go have yourselves a great, female-bonding kind of afternoon. I'll be fine—promise!"

He waited until she had left the bedroom before he turned to look at himself in the mirror that hung above the bureau. "Liar," he told his reflection, then headed for the kitchen to make a solitary lunch. "Like it said in that magazine Jill read, Hackett— you can do it. Remember? You just have to *try harder.*"

Jill entered the house through the back door, having said goodbye to Barbara, who had been wonderful about having her evening canceled by Ted's unexpected arrival.

Barbara had been wonderful about a lot of things, a real brick, actually, and Jill was grateful to her friend, even if Barbara had eventually let it slip that she'd met a man at the corner grocery store just that morning as she did errands for her mother, and he had asked her out for tonight.

As a matter of fact, Barbara had been looking for a way to tell her friend that *she* wanted to break their ice-skating date!

"Right in the produce section, Jill," Barbara had told her happily. "Just the way they say it happens in those magazines—although I never would have believed it if Pete hadn't reached for *exactly* the same cantaloupe I was aiming for. I mean, it was like *fate* had intervened or something. Anyway, I really don't mind canceling out tonight if *you* really don't mind—which I guess you don't, because who would want to go ice-skating alongside of a bunch of teenagers on a Saturday night if they had a man around? *I* sure wouldn't, even if it was my idea in the first place. Did I mention that Pete has green eyes? I mean, *green!* Just like the 'go' light on a traffic light!"

Jill was smiling as she deposited the badly tarnished silver tray she had purchased at the antique show on the kitchen table. Ted would probably laugh at her for buying the thing, but it had been such a bargain even if it was slightly dented on one side, and she was convinced it would look fine once it was polished.

And speaking of Ted, she mused to herself, cocking her head to one side, listening for some hint as to whether or not he was in the house... He hadn't been out back, although both their cars were there, neatly washed, their paint and chrome gleaming in the late afternoon sun.

He wasn't taking a shower, she knew, or else she would be hearing the pipes knock as they always did when the faucets were turned on upstairs, and the television set wasn't blaring with the Saturday afternoon baseball game.

So where was he?

"Ted? Are you in here?" She called his name again as she passed through the dining room and peeked into the living room before heading upstairs.

A minute later she was back in the kitchen, still none the wiser as to her husband's whereabouts. Shrugging, she opened the refrigerator, sticking her head inside to discover if Ted had left any of the cold cuts she had planned to serve for dinner or if he had eaten them all for lunch, the way he had done the last time he was home.

She had long ago given up fixing him a cooked meal his first day home, for they never seemed to get around to eating it. Saturdays, she remembered now, were entirely too full of "other things" for either of them to concentrate on food. Sundays she would fix his favorite, roast beef, and then send some of the leftovers back with him to San Francisco.

Jillian had pulled open the meat drawer, to see if the sliced baked ham had survived Ted's lunch, when suddenly she saw it.

"Is that dog food?" she questioned out loud, reaching for the opened half-empty can clumsily wrapped inside a plastic sandwich bag. "That's ridiculous. It can't be!" She closed her eyes, then opened them and looked again. "*Dog* food?"

Closing the refrigerator door, she cast her eyes around the floor, searching for evidence of a dog. She found it at last in the pantry, just beside the back door—two small brand-new metal dishes, one holding water and the other containing the rather disgusting looking remnants of the same stuff that was at the moment smelling up her clean refrigerator.

"A *dog?*" She repeated aloud, feeling stupid. "Ted found a *dog?*"

She looked down at the dishes again and corrected herself. "No. Ted didn't *find* a dog. Ted *bought* a dog. At least it's a small dog, if it couldn't finish a single can of food. I guess I should be grateful for small favors. But Ted has definitely bought a dog, and he bought dishes for the dog and he bought dog food for the dog. Now all he needs is a doghouse for the dog—one big enough to hold the *two* of them, because the man isn't sleeping in here tonight! If I let him *live* until tonight, that is!"

She heard a slight commotion at the front door and returned to the kitchen in time to see Ted being dragged down the hallway from the entrance way by a huge black *horse.*

"Whoa, Sinbad! Whoa!" Ted commanded, his right arm looking as if it were about to be pulled from its socket as he yanked on a thick red-leather leash.

But the black horse wasn't in a "whoaing" mood.

He just kept coming, not halting until his four huge paws made contact with the recently waxed tile floor, at which time all four paws shot out in different directions, leaving Sinbad on his belly at her feet, his huge head inches from her toes.

"Hello, Sinbad," Jillian said as calmly as she could. "Gobble up any nice mailmen lately?"

Ted collapsed onto the floor just inside the kitchen, smiling up at Jillian as he let go of the leash and began shaking his hand, as if to get the circulation started in it once more. "Hi, Slugger! You'll never guess what I did today."

"Yes, I will, *darling*," she answered, taking a single prudent step away from Sinbad's jaws. "You went crazy today. Your mental train jumped its tracks. You lost one of your oars in the water. You slipped a few shingles off your roof. *You bought a horse!*"

Ted sat cross-legged on the floor, patting Sinbad's broad back. "Don't exaggerate, Jill," he said, still smiling, just as if it had not yet occurred to him that he was in deep trouble. "Sinbad's not all that big. He's still a puppy, for crying out loud—only ten months old. He's part shepherd and part Labrador—mostly lab, I think. But he's got the disposition of a cuddly teddy bear, honest!"

"Uh-huh," Jillian answered, watching as Sinbad struggled to rise, only to sprawl on the floor once more, his rump landing on Ted's leg.

"I got him at the pound," Ted continued, not that Jillian had asked any questions. No, she just stood there, her fists propped against her hips, looking at him the same way his mother had the day he brought home a stray cat, swearing it had followed him all the way from school—which would have been a pretty neat trick if a six-week-old kitten really could walk twelve blocks on its own.

"He's been neutered, he's trained, he's had all his shots," he went on quickly, adding, "and he doesn't have any fleas."

He considered that last bit to be important, especially since the kitten had brought a whole generation of fleas into his childhood home, to breed in the living room carpet. He'd had to give up his allowance for six months in order to pay the exterminator bill.

"Uh-huh," Jillian answered, archly lifting one eyebrow as Sinbad swung his big head around and began gnawing on the shoelace in Ted's left sneaker.

Ted pushed the dog's head away. "Stop that, Sinbad! You've already wolfed down nearly two cans of dog food. You can't be hungry any more."

He looked up at Jillian, smiling sheepishly. "He's got a great appetite, hon'."

"Uh-huh."

Ted winced. "You hate him, don't you?"

"No, Ted. I don't hate Sinbad."

"You hate me?"

"No, Ted. I don't hate you, either."

Ted pushed Sinbad away and scrambled to his feet. He and the dog had been out for a run—Sinbad leading the way for most of it—and he was sweaty and overheated. But he wasn't brain dead. Jillian was angry.

"Let me take a wild stab at this, Slugger, okay? You're angry that I didn't ask you first? Is that it? That I didn't consult with you the way a good husband should?"

Jillian nodded. "It may have taken you a while, but I knew you'd get it sooner or later. That's why I married you—because you're so wonderfully swift on the uptake."

"Nasty, nasty. But I suppose I deserved that. I'm sorry, Slugger. Next time I'll ask—promise." He kissed her cheek as he walked past her to pull open the refrigerator and pull out a can of iced tea. "Phew! Did something die in here?"

"No, darling. Sinbad's dog food is in the refrigerator, wrapped ever so neatly by his master—who stuck a plastic sandwich bag over it, as if the can were wearing a *hat!*"

"Whoops." Ted quickly pulled out a can of iced tea and closed the door. "Guess I'll have to find a better way to store it, huh?"

"Good thought," Jillian answered, watching as Sinbad finally found his "sea legs" and struggled to his feet. He came over to her and began sniffing at her knees, then sat down, looking up at her as if to say "Hi, do you live here, too?"

Ted slipped an arm around Jillian's shoulders. "I'm really sorry I didn't ask first, Slugger, but I took a drive and I saw the pound and, well, I just succumbed to impulse, that's all. You told me you were lonely here alone, remember? I thought that if you had Sinbad here with you it would help with the loneliness. I think we even talked about getting a dog, if I remember correctly. We always talk about kids and dogs. Since we aren't planning on any babies for a while, I thought I'd get us started off with Sinbad here."

Jillian gritted her teeth. "Uh-huh."

"Back to monosyllables are we?" Ted looked down at Sinbad, who was now lying on the floor, his black eyes watching the two of them steadily, as if he knew his continued presence in the house was in question. "I could have gotten a puppy, but I figured Sinbad could be a sort of watchdog, you know, and protect you when I'm out of town."

"With the disposition of a cuddly teddy bear? Tell me, Ted, how is he going to protect me—or is it your plan that Sinbad *drool* any prospective robbers to death?"

Ted looked down at the table and saw the tarnished silver tray. "Yeah, well," he said, hefting the heavy piece with one hand, "if Sinbad can't hold them back, just give them this. It's got to be worth at least three dollars."

"Two seventy-five," Jillian snapped, "and at least *my* purchase won't eat us out of house and home."

That last crack was beneath her and she knew it, but she felt she had to say something.

More angry with herself than with Ted, she snatched the tray away from him, but didn't get a good grip and it slipped from her fingers, landing on the tile floor with a mighty crash.

Sinbad immediately began to whimper like the overgrown puppy he was, and tried to climb Ted's leg, his back paws slipping on the floor so that he ended by falling in a heap at Jillian's feet.

"Oh, you poor darling!" Jillian exclaimed, instantly contrite, bending down to comfort the frightened animal. "Did that nasty, old tray scare you? Shame on you, Ted! You should have made sure I had a good grip on it before you let go. Now look what's happened. Sinbad is trembling!"

Sinbad, who seemed to know opportunity when it patted him on the head, began licking Jillian's hand, his soulful black eyes openly adoring her. "Oh, brother," she said, sighing. "Damn you, Theodore J-for-Joseph Hackett—I think I'm in love."

That evening, after scratching outside the closed bedroom door and yowling a time or two, Sinbad slept on the carpet at the bottom of Jillian and Ted's bed, an accepted member of the family.

Chapter Ten

"In November? What in blue blazes are you going to do in Sea Isle City in *November?* I'm telling you, Jill, living in lala land all these months has done something dangerous to Ted's brain. Melted it, maybe. It'll probably rain the entire weekend."

Jillian sat down on the edge of the bed, the butter-yellow sweater she had been about to pack in her suitcase still in her hands. "Or snow," she said dully, stroking the soft lamb's wool. "We had flurries here last Tuesday, remember?" She shook her head. "I don't know, Barb. I think Ted wants to prove that a beach is not a beach is not a beach."

"Huh? You want to run that one by me one more

time? I think I missed something important along the way."

Jillian began picking a few stray black hairs—Sinbad hairs—from the sweater. Why Sinbad was shedding in November Jillian would never begin to understand, but, then, she also tried not to delve too deeply into the dog's unbelievable passion for mashed potatoes.

"Simple, Barb. It doesn't snow on the sunny beaches of California. It's supposed to get cold and damp sometime, but it hasn't yet so far this year. I'm telling you, Barb, even the climate is out to get me. When Ted phoned last night he told me that he and Steve had borrowed some wet suits and gone body surfing in the afternoon. *Surfing!* I expect to see him whizzing around our back alley on roller blades any day now."

Barbara, who was lying on her stomach across the bed, cupped her chin in her hands. "I don't know, Jill. I think Ted would look cute in a helmet and knee pads. But I can see where this is heading. Ted's still doing his 'let's think about living in California' bit, isn't he?"

Jillian nodded, sighing. "He doesn't even try to hide it any more. It's so unfair, Barb! When I go out to San Francisco we play in the surf and go to the theater on half-price tickets he finds somewhere and visit all these lovely places...but when Ted flies home all we ever seem to do is caulk that miserable, leaky shower stall, wash and hang the storm windows or get the backyard ready for winter. There's not a whole hell of a lot of romance in mulching roses, Barb—and damn little time for smelling them."

Barb rolled off the bed, to stand staring down at her friend. "Oh, boy—using cuss words now, are we? This is more serious than I thought. Please don't tell me the honeymoon is over, Jill. With my own wedding only six months away, I'd hate to think real life intrudes this fast after the ceremony."

"Of course it doesn't, Barb," Jillian hastened to assure her friend. Ever since that momentous day in the produce section of the local grocery store, Barbara and Pete had indulged in a whirlwind courtship—leading up to the diamond ring he had presented to her on her birthday in October.

"And you and Pete aren't going to be living on opposite sides of the country. When he drops his wet towel on the bed you can just read him the riot act there and then, not grin and bear it because you're only going to see him for forty-eight hours and you don't want to spend any of that time being a nag."

She stood and carefully placed the sweater in the suitcase before zipping the lid closed. "And our honeymoon is *not* over. It—it's just beginning to fray around the edges a little."

Jillian pulled the suitcase from the bed, took one last look around the bedroom, then led the way to the staircase, blinking back stupid tears. She didn't want Barbara to see how truly distressed she was, how very much she was dreading this weekend at the New Jersey shore.

As they reached the bottom of the staircase, Sinbad raised his huge head from the dining room carpet, looked at her sadly, then gave out a single, small whimper, as if he knew she was going out of his life for two whole days and nights.

"Oh—don't you start in on me now, you overgrown ball of fur! I've got problems enough of my own," Jillian exclaimed, brushing past him and into the kitchen, quickly checking to make sure she had turned off the coffeepot. "Honestly, Barb, sometimes I think my whole life has become one big guilt trip."

"Well, you don't have to worry about Sinbad, Jill," Barbara said, dropping onto one of the kitchen chairs. "Pete and I are going to take him for runs each morning and Mom will probably spoil him rotten, feeding him treats. Does he still go wild over mashed potatoes?"

"Strawberry yogurt is his latest love, now that Ted has embarked the two of us on some California health kick," Jillian muttered under her breath, searching in the cabinet for the aspirin bottle. She was getting a terrible headache. "But don't give him any. I don't think it's good for him. Oh—look at the time! If I'm going to get to the airport in time to meet Ted's flight I'll have to leave now. Barb—wish me luck?"

She downed two aspirin, then dived into a single arm of her coat as Barbara held it up for her. "My keys! Where in blazes did I put my keys?"

With a hand to her mouth, she cast her frantic gaze around the kitchen, desperately trying to remember where she had put the car keys when she had arrived home from school.

She stood very still, trying to concentrate, her coat nearly falling off her shoulder. She had stayed after classes, to help Tommy Easterman with his long division, then raced to the store to lay in some extra cans of Sinbad's favorite dog food before stopping to retrieve Ted's winter coat from the cleaners.

"That's it! Ted's coat!" Water spilled from her glass as she banged it down on the counter instead of putting it in the sink where it belonged. "I almost forgot to pack Ted's coat!" Slipping her other arm into the remaining sleeve, she flew into the dining room, to see Ted's plastic-wrapped coat lying on the table, the car keys beside it. "That's right. I put the keys and the coat together so I wouldn't forget. So how did I forget that?"

Clutching the coat to her, she spun in a half circle to glare at her friend. "I can't tell you how I hate this, Barb. Half of Ted's wardrobe is here and the other half is in San Francisco—except when he brings it home in a bag for me to wash for him. I'm thinking of hanging out a sign saying that I take in wash. Jillian Hackett's laundry, home cooking and sex. We deliver!"

Barb leaned against the doorjamb, smiling at her friend. "You'd have a bumper business there, Jill—especially with that 'sex' bit."

Jillian's bottom lip began to quiver, a sure indication to both Barbara and herself that a bout of tears was imminent. She ran a hand through her hair, wincing as she remembered that she had given in to impulse earlier in the week and had it cut to chin length—without telling Ted.

Tears stung her eyes and she collapsed into a nearby chair. "My hair! Oh, Barb—he's going to hate it. Absolutely *hate* it. Last night—" her voice broke slightly "—just last night on the telephone Ted told me how he'd been dreaming about my hair spread out on his pillow beside him."

Barb coughed behind the hand she'd raised to hide her smile. "He can still have that. You could dribble hair anywhere he wants it, on his pillow, in the tub drain, in his vegetable soup. Or did you forget to ask the beautician to give you the cut hair—in a doggie bag, or something?"

Jillian tried to force a smile. She knew what her friend was doing. She was trying to show her how stupid it was to be overreacting the way she was. And she *was* overreacting. She wiped at her eyes, then raised her hands in mock surrender.

"Okay, okay, so maybe I'm unraveling a little here. But I'll be fine, Barb—honest. Just be a pal and head me in the general direction of the back door, all right? Time and Lombard Airways flight arrivals wait for no woman, even if she doesn't quite have her act together."

"*You?*" Barbara mocked, "The queen of organization? The woman who schedules everything from housecleaning to tooth flossing? The lady who believes neatness is the Eleventh Commandment? Oh, never say so, Jill. You'll undermine my belief in an orderly world system."

"Put a sock in it, okay?" Jillian shot back, giving in to laughter. "You're beginning to sound like Ted. He says I can't be spontaneous." Her smile broadened. "I told him that was ridiculous."

Barbara handed Jillian the ring holding the car keys and pushed her through the kitchen, heading her in the direction of the back door. "You did, did you? What did you say?"

Her hand gripping the doorknob, Jillian took hold of the handle of the small suitcase Barbara thrust at her and answered brightly, "I can too be spontaneous, I told him—if only he'd *call* first!"

"That's our girl!" Barbara called after her as Jillian made her way to the car. "Now forget San Francisco and wet towels and laundry—and go have fun! You deserve it."

Jillian turned back toward the house to see Barbara and Sinbad standing in the open doorway. "I do, don't I? I love you, Barbara McAllister!" she shouted *spontaneously*. "You too, you silly mutt! See you Sunday night."

* * *

Ted took a drink from his glass of chilled California white wine and frowned. It was nearly midnight and he was in the small sitting room in their rented Sea Isle City condo. It was nearly midnight and he was *alone* in the small sitting room in their rented Sea Isle City condo.

"What in hell am I doing here?" he asked himself in a near whisper, watching as the quasi-log fire he had laid earlier in the stone corner fireplace flickered its last cheery flame, then died.

Mentally, he reviewed the trip from the ABE airport, down the Pennsylvania Turnpike, across the Walt Whitman Bridge and traveling the length of the Atlantic City Expressway, to the 7S exit, and beyond.

Jillian had barely spoken throughout the three-hour trip, except to answer his questions about Sinbad and her students, and whether or not she'd paid the water bill in time to take advantage of the early payment discount.

She hadn't been quiet because of hunger, for he had specifically asked if she had eaten something before she left the house and she'd told him she'd downed a couple of things just before going out the door. As he had eaten on the plane, he hadn't pushed her.

Maybe he should have. She had lost weight these past three weeks, since last he'd seen her.

Lost weight and cut her hair.

He hadn't said anything. Oh, no, even though he didn't really like her new hairstyle, he'd kept his mouth shut about it. Until she asked. Why did she have to ask? And what had he said that was all that terrible? "'It's nice, Slugger, but I think I like it better long,'" he repeated now, aloud. "That's all I said. So how did that simple statement escalate into World War III?"

He looked toward the door to the single bedroom. The *closed* door to the bedroom, where Jillian had retreated after giving him a pithy lecture on spontaneity, telling him that cutting her hair had been a spontaneous act and he was the one who said she should try it some time. *Spontaneity?* What the devil did spontaneity have to do with having one's hair chopped off, anyway?

He deposited the wineglass on the end table and sat forward, his elbows propped on his knees, to run his hands through his hair in exasperation. He'd held out such high hopes for this weekend. Coming back here to Sea Isle City, to the site of their short honeymoon, taking Jillian away from that damnable house and its leaking faucets and neatly cataloged unpaid bills... renewing the early carefree days of their whirlwind courtship.

It had seemed like such a good idea, before reality had come crashing in on them.

"Ted?"

He lifted his head and looked toward the bedroom, to see Jillian standing in a small spill of light coming from somewhere behind her. She was dressed in the full-length ivory silk negligée she had worn on their wedding night, and he could clearly see the outline of her body beneath the sheer material.

She was so beautiful, and he loved her. He loved her so much.

"Are you all right, Ted?" she asked, slowly advancing into the living room. "I mean, you can't be very comfortable out here. Don't you want to come into bed?"

He gave her a lopsided smile, patting the cushion beside him invitingly. "That had been my original intention, yes. But I think we'd better talk first, if you're in the mood?"

"Talk?" Jillian's voice, he noted, came out in a small squeak, then she sighed. "Oh, all right. I suppose so. But if we're going to talk, I think I'd better sit over here, in this chair, away from temptation."

"Safely out of the way of my tremendous male attraction?" Ted teased, leaning back against the cushions and already beginning to feel better about their chances for an enjoyable weekend.

"No, darling," she answered sweetly, lowering herself into the chair that faced the couch across the modern glass-and-blond-wood coffee table. "To keep me from beaning you if you look at me one more time with that innocent 'Who? Me?' expression on your face and ask, 'Is something wrong, Slugger?'"

Ted picked up his wineglass, and discovering it to be empty, rose to refill it while at the same time pouring a glassful for Jillian. "I'm sorry about that crack about your hair, Slugger," he said, sure that his remark had been what had set her off in the first place. "Besides, I'm getting used to it now. You look almost pixieish, if that's the right word for it. It was just a shock when I first saw you, that's all."

She took the wineglass even as she waved away his apology. "That was my fault, Ted. I overreacted—and I should have told you I was getting my hair cut. Not asked you—but told you. Anyway, as I can't glue it back on again, I imagine we'll both have to learn to live with it for a while."

"Deal," Ted agreed, happy to have the subject out of the way. "Now, Slugger—why don't you tell me what's really on your mind?"

"I don't think so." She looked away from him. "You won't like it."

He gave a short bark of laughter, mostly to cover his nervousness. Something was wrong, and he had the oddest feeling that it wasn't something simple, like a leaky faucet that needed repairing. "Are you going to tell me one of those old jokes, Slugger? You know—'Honey, I have a little bad news. The garage burned down.' Then I ask, 'Oh, really, how did that happen?' and you reply, 'Sparks from the *house!*'"

"Very funny, Ted. Almost as funny as hearing you say that the good news is that you got a promotion and a raise, but the bad news is that your company will be paying out that new, higher salary in San Francisco. But never mind that. To answer your question, the house is fine. Sinbad is find. It—it's me. I'm what's not *fine*. To be perfectly blunt about the thing—I'm a mess!"

Suddenly Ted was on his knees beside Jillian's chair. "Slugger—honey—are you trying to tell me something? Are we going to have a baby?"

"A *baby?*" she countered in obvious surprise, shaking her head. "No, darling, we are not having a baby. As an elementary-school-level mathematics teacher, might I point out that conception is only one of the possibilities whose odds lengthen in direct proportion to the number of miles separating the husband and wife in question. But only one of them," she added softly, so very quietly that he barely heard her.

But he did hear her. "What else do the odds lengthen on, Slugger?" he asked, remembering the figures she had quoted him on the numbers of so-called "commuter marriages."

Had she read another article, one less optimistic? Or was he blind and Jillian truly wasn't handling their circumstances as well as he had been trying to tell himself she had been? Had she been coping better lately, as he had thought, or had she only learned to hide her unhappiness better?

She sighed. "I don't really know, Ted. And I don't want to learn. In other words—I think it's time we called this thing off."

His heart dropped to his feet. "Call it off? Are you talking about a separation?"

"*No!*" Jillian shook her heat vehemently, then looked at her husband in dawning apprehension. "That is—unless you are," she added softly. "Are you? I'm not. Besides," she concluded, beginning to smile nervously, "how could we tell if we were separated? We're hardly together as it is."

"Very funny," Ted responded, visibly relaxing. "But if neither of us is talking about calling off our marriage, Slugger—then would you please tell me what in hell we *are* talking about?"

"What I'm talking about is the fact that I want us to begin living together all the time, not just on alternate weekends. I want us to argue about whose turn it is to take out the garbage and whether we watch sports on television or a game show, and go food shopping together and even be *bored* together. I want us to begin being *married.*"

Ted sat back on the floor and spread his hands in confusion. "Are you saying we aren't really married because we don't argue about the garbage? Slugger, that's—that's *garbage!*"

"Is it?" she flung back at him. "Then can you explain to me why I feel like the biggest reason we get together is to make love? That I feel like the only conversations we have are about when we'll meet and where we'll meet, and in the end it doesn't matter anyway because all we seem to do is make love anyway, even if neither of us is really in the mood—because we're together and we're supposed to be making love? That is why we're here, isn't it, spending money we should be saving for our future—to make love?"

Ted's gaze slid away from hers. "So you feel that way, too?" he asked quietly, feeling equal portions of guilt and relief wash over him. "And don't look at me that way. I'm admitting it, Slugger—there are times when I feel like we're just playing house. It was exciting for a while—damned exciting—but we're not kids. There *is* more to marriage than sex."

Jillian slipped from the chair, to sit on the floor alongside Ted. "Not that the sex is *all* that bad, of course," she said, giggling faintly as she leaned her head against his shoulder.

"No—it's not all that bad," he agreed, sliding an arm around her shoulders. "As a matter of fact, it's pretty damn marvelous, which is why I thought having a weekend away from the house was a good idea. But you didn't think so, did you, Slugger?"

He felt her head move in the negative. "I thought you were sort of telling me without telling me that the house and Sinbad and our bills were making you feel trapped and you just wanted to make love, as if we were lovers and not really married—when I was already wanting so much to feel *more* married."

She pushed her head up, to look into his eyes. "My imagination was working overtime again, wasn't it? Sometimes I'm so stupid! That's why we shouldn't have these separations. They give me too much time alone to think up ridiculous ideas. And I used to believe I was so *sane!*"

He kissed her forehead, easing away the lines of worry he hated to see there. "You are sane, Slugger. It's our situation that's insane. We're living separate lives, on opposite sides of the country, with time out for stolen moments during which we try to cram as much life as possible into the hours we're together. I think, to be honest about it all, that we've been killing ourselves trying to prove that this ridiculous arrangement can work."

"So now you agree that we can't go on like this for another year and a half? Because if I can't get a teaching position in San Francisco, it will be another year and a half until you are back in Allentown."

"No, I'm not saying that," Ted told her, helping her to her feet and steering her toward the bedroom, for the living room was rapidly becoming chilly. "I'm just saying that we have to stop trying so hard to be the perfect couple. The couple that never fights, the couple that spends every moment madly in love and loving. Admit it, Jill, that weekend last month when you had that bad head cold—you were wishing me in California and not in Allentown, arriving with a yen for roast beef, clean laundry and a romantic interlude."

She sat on the side of the mattress, then slipped her feet under the covers as he joined her on the opposite side of the bed. "I could have lived without you that weekend," she said, grinning. "Although I did appreciate the fact that you walked Sinbad so that I could stay in bed. But what about the weekend you had me come to San Francisco—the weekend you were studying for that written exam? You couldn't have wanted to take me to dinner and a movie. But you did, because our time together is precious, and we seem to believe we must fill every minute of it with memories that will sustain us while we're apart."

Ted relaxed against the pillows, feeling more comfortable, more relaxed than he had in months. "You know what it is, Slugger?" he asked, coming to a conclusion. "We knew we had to try harder, and being overachievers we've taken it a step farther—and we're trying *too* hard. I don't know why I didn't see it before." He turned to look at her. "So—do you want to pack up and go home?"

Jillian reached out to trace a design on his chest with her fingertips. "I don't know. We *are* here. We're talking about things that matter, with no pressure on us anymore, no feeling that we have to be making love every moment and acting as if we don't get on each other's nerves once in a while. Tell me—are you really beginning to like my hair this way?"

He pulled her closer. "Slugger, I don't care if you shave your head—just promise me that we'll always be open with each other from now on. We're in this together, remember? Now why don't we both get a good night's sleep?"

He gave her a short, satisfying kiss, then lay back and looked up at the ceiling as she snuggled her head into the hollow beneath his shoulder blade.

Five minutes passed as he watched the moonlight weave patterns on the ceiling and listened to the muffled sound of the waves breaking on the beach outside the condo. Then he suddenly became aware of the fact that Jillian was no longer lying quite still.

Her right hand was drifting toward the waistband of the jogging shorts he had donned earlier, when they'd first arrived at the condo.

Her fingertips skimmed the skin along the upper edge of the elastic band, then dipped inside it, traveling lower, tracing small circles on his suddenly sensitized skin.

"Jilly?" he questioned her huskily, for now her teeth were nipping lightly at his chest, her warm breath teasing his senses.

"Hmm?" she replied, easing her hip against him, one long leg crossed over his, her knee insinuating itself between his thighs.

"You don't have to do this, you know," he said, wishing he could regulate his breathing better, hide his obvious reaction to her lovemaking. "We've agreed that there's to be no pressure on either of us any more. We don't have to make love simply because we're in Sea Isle City or simply because we haven't seen each other for two weeks."

She sat up, quickly lifting the hem of her nightgown over her head, tossed the discarded garment to the floor and then knelt in front of him on the mattress.

"No, we don't, do we, darling," she said, grinning "and for some strange reason that freedom only makes me want you more than ever. Isn't that *wonderful?*"

He reached up to cup her breasts in his hands, to glory in the sight of her in the moonlight. "I'd say that's better than wonderful, wife. *You're* better than wonderful. Now—come here!"

Chapter Eleven

"Christmas Eve, of course. Doesn't everybody?"

"Christmas Eve? You've *got* to be kidding! I always knew there was something strange about you, Theodore Hackett. Christmas *morning*."

"I am not kidding, Slugger, and I'll thank you to remember that this is the love of your life you're speaking to. Christmas Eve! It's easier."

"Don't even think about it! Christmas *morning!* It's traditional!"

"Traditional, is it? Ah, now there's a word I've come to know well this year." Ted then rolled his eyes, aware he was lucky he and Jillian were having this conversation long-distance.

"Look, Slugger, how about a compromise? We'll open one gift apiece on Christmas Eve and save the rest of them for Christmas morning. It's not your tradition or my tradition, but it will be *our* tradition. Is it a deal?"

There was a slight pause at the other end of the line, then Jillian's soft laughter filtered through to him and he relaxed. "You've missed your calling, darling," he heard her say. "You should have been in the diplomatic corps. And, yes—it's a deal. Now let's discuss Christmas dinner. What are you used to—turkey or roast beef?"

"If I say my folks always ate roast beef on Christmas, I'd be willing to lay odds that your family has always had turkey and all the trimmings. So—how about tuna-fish salad? We won't be stepping on anyone's traditions and we don't even have to use knives to eat it. At the rate this discussion is going, I think we might both be safer that way."

"Very funny, Ted. There will be coal in *somebody's* stocking this year for sure. Tell you what—I'll surprise you, okay? Have you gotten the final word on when you'll be coming home? It would be wonderful if you could be here in time to help decorate the tree."

"I won't know about my flight until the last minute," he told Jillian as he leaned over the balcony and waved at Nicky Hunter as she approached the apartment building, a mesh grocery bag loaded with raw vegetables slung over her shoulder, her long, tanned legs bare to the top of her thighs. How could it be December twenty-second? He felt as if it were no later than the middle of autumn.

"I can only narrow it down to sometime early Christmas Eve night, hon'. All I can tell you is to hang the mistletoe and put a candle in the window. I'll grab a cab at the airport, so you won't have to worry about picking me up."

Jillian sighed once more, but this time she sounded contented. "Our very first Christmas together. Oh, Ted, I can hardly wait! Maybe it will snow, although we haven't had many white Christmases lately."

"As long as the white stuff holds off until we've taxied in to the terminal. I'm not looking forward to spending Christmas Eve munching stale candy bars in some airport lounge in the Midwest."

He heard a knock on the glass door behind him and turned to see Steve motioning that he wanted to use the telephone. "Hey, Slugger—I've got to go. Steve has to break it to his parents that he drew the short straw and won't be getting home until after the New Year, when I get back. That's why I brought the telephone out onto the balcony. I feel kinda guilty—not that I'm going to trade places with him—but us married guys do deserve a break now and then. Lombard Airways, the airline with a heart. Now, tell me how much you love me, Slugger, and I'll see you in two days."

* * *

The entire house smelled of Christmas, from the handmade cinnamon broom Jillian had found in a local craft shop and hung in the entranceway to the woodsy smell emanating from the small, still undecorated balsam fir Christmas tree in the living room, to the tins of chocolate chip, buttery cutout and gingerbread cookies that sat on the buffet in the dining room.

There were electric candles burning in every window, not just the single one Ted had requested.

A large, jolly, lighted plastic Santa Claus figure, one gloved hand raised in greeting, smiled at passersby from its perch on the front steps.

Strings of glowing red-and-green colored lights edged the doorway and the double-hung windows that fronted on the street.

An antique hand-carved crèche passed down from Jillian's great-grandmother sat in its usual place of honor on a table in the living room, the figures nestled amid a bower of freshly cut greens.

It was Christmas Eve and everything was lovely; almost perfect.

The pity of the thing was that Jillian wasn't there to delight in any of it.

Jillian, thanks to a freak ice storm that had slipped into the Allentown area without warning about an hour before the school children were to be dismissed at noon to begin their Christmas vacation, was sitting a mile away in the crowded emergency room of Allentown Hospital.

At the moment she was glaring at her grossly swollen ankle as it rested on the chair in front of her, an ice bag tied to her foot. A misstep had sent her crashing to the pavement as she made her way to the parking lot, her arms laden with small Christmas gifts from her students.

She sniffed at the sleeve of her favorite pale yellow angora sweater and grimaced. Every other mother had seemed to have decided that cologne made the perfect "teacher present," and Jillian knew she smelled like the perfume counter at any of the local department stores—for at least two of the "presents" had shattered in the fall, showering her with scent.

She looked through the glass double doors, to see that it was pitch-dark outside. Glancing at her watch, she grimaced again. Five o'clock! No wonder it was dark! She had been waiting for almost four hours, for the emergency room was packed with patients like her, who either had come to grief on the slippery pavements or were here thanks to the dozens of "fender benders" that were occurring at nearly every intersection.

She'd leave if she could. Ted could be arriving at home any minute, and he would be frantic to find the house dark except for the Christmas lights—which she had attached to a timer—and her nowhere to be found.

But she couldn't leave. Her car was still in the parking lot at the school, for one thing—as one of the other teachers had volunteered to drive her to the hospital—and for another thing, she couldn't bear to put any weight on her ankle.

She knew, because she'd tried, and it had hurt like hell.

The door to the treatment room opened yet again and Jillian leaned forward expectantly, only to listen while the nurse read someone else's name from the paper she held in her hand.

Jillian watched as a little girl no more than three was carried into the treatment room by her mother, the child's huge blue eyes bright with fever as she rested one reddened cheek against her mother's shoulder.

"Well, I can't be angry about that," Jillian muttered into her sweater collar, then leaned her head back against the wall behind her chair, to stare up at the oddly pathetic looking string of twinkling Christmas lights someone had strung at ceiling level.

Flashes of the Christmas she had spent on the couch, too ill with tonsillitis to play with her new toys, appeared before her eyes and she hoped the little girl would feel better soon.

Jillian had always had a "thing" for holidays, now that she thought about it. Chicken pox on her fifth birthday... a black eye from an errant baseball the day before her confirmation... that stomach virus the first New Year's Eve her mother had actually allowed her to date...

"Jill? Jilly! Are you all right? Good Lord, girl, what have you done now? Mom gave me your message as soon as I got home and I rushed right over—the ice is all gone now, as fast as it came. Stupid weather... but I had a devil of a time finding a parking place. It looks like the whole world has spent the afternoon falling all over the streets. What's broken? Your *ankle?* Oh, brother! What a mess! Pete's boss slid into a telephone pole—but only broke a headlight. No wonder birds fly south for the winter."

"Hi, Barb," Jillian answered calmly as her friend collapsed into the chair beside her, her cheeks flushed nearly as red as the balls on the small plastic Christmas tree stuck drunkenly in a corner of the emergency room, her brand-new rabbit fur jacket falling off her shoulders. "Thanks for coming over. Is Ted home yet? I wanted to call, but I don't want him to hear this over the phone."

"I know. Mom said I wasn't to say anything to him if I saw him. But, no, there aren't any lights on at your place except for good, old Santa and the others, so I suppose his flight didn't get in yet."

"Well, thank heaven for small favors. With any luck, I still might beat him home and he'll never have to know. I want to surprise him with what I found in those boxes he stored in the basement."

Barbara looked down at Jillian's swollen ankle and shook her head. "I don't get it, Jilly. It isn't as if you're going to be able to keep something like this a secret. Ted strikes me as a pretty smart guy—although I doubt it would take a brain surgeon to figure out that something is very wrong once he sees the cast on your leg."

Jillian sat up a little in her chair, bristling. "Nobody said there's going to be a cast on my leg, Barb. Don't be so pessimistic, for crying out loud. I may just have sprained it. I'm still waiting to hear the results of the X ray."

Barbara shook her head, still staring at Jillian's ankle. "Oh, it's broken all right," she said, then sighed, pointing at her friend's foot. "See where the skin is getting all black and blue—right there, just below the ice pack? That's a break. You can count on it."

"Well, thank you, Dr. McAllister, for that stunningly brilliant, not to mention *scientific* diagnosis. If only you could have arrived sooner, you would have saved all those silly doctors the bother of X-raying my ankle. I wonder how Sinbad is doing. I'm usually home by now. The poor little fella must be starving."

"Yeah, right. That mutt could live off his own fat for a month." Barbara slipped her arms out of her jacket and looked around the crowded room. "Jolly here, isn't it? Do you know how much longer you're going to be, Jilly? I mean, did they give you a number or anything? Like they do at the deli section in the supermarket?"

Jillian was saved from having to answer Barbara's question as a nurse popped her head through the doorway and called out, "Hackett? The orthopedic surgeon will see you now."

"Orthopedic surgeon? Oh, it's broken all right," Barbara pronounced fatalistically, helping Jillian to her feet. "They don't waste time, these surgeons. If it were only a sprain, you'd be talking to a physician's assistant."

Jillian leaned heavily against Barbara and began hopping toward the doorway. "You know what, Barb? You watch too many soap operas, with all their pseudo doctors and long-lost amnesiacs."

Barbara supported Jillian's elbow and helped her through the doorway. "Okay—so maybe you and I never met anyone who had amnesia," she said, smiling at the nurse. "But it happens. Believe me."

Jillian gritted her teeth as hopping sent lightning bolts of pain shooting through her bruised ankle. "I don't know much about amnesia, Barb—but much as it kills me to say this, I think you're right about one thing. This ankle has *got* to be broken. Nothing else could hurt this much."

Ted stepped from the cab, smiling. The old house looked great—cheery, welcoming—and almost an exact match of Barbara's house, except that there was no Santa on Barb's small front porch, but a grinning, top-hatted snowman instead.

He paid the driver, then stood on the pavement for a moment, his uniform hat tipped back on his head, and looked up and down the street, taking in the sight of so many houses all decked out for Christmas, and at last felt a measurable measure of Christmas cheer entering his spirit.

This was all that had been missing—a street lined with bare winter trees, a definite nip in the air, frost on the ground and old brick houses outlined in colored lights.

He remembered that when he left San Francisco it had been raining. Not snowing—but raining. And damp and foggy as well. There was, he decided, something to be said for living in Pennsylvania—the definite changing of the four seasons.

Hefting his wardrobe bag over his shoulder and picking up his flight bag, Ted briskly climbed the four shallow steps to the front porch and slid his key into the lock.

He had only had time to notice the homey smell of cinnamon in the air before a low growl reached his ears. Sinbad was standing at the opposite end of the hallway, his feet planted firmly on the carpet, his rather large, pointed teeth bared, the hair on his back standing up like an ebony ruff and his tail standing out straight.

If Ted had been a burglar, he decided, he would have been halfway out of town by now—his own tail cravenly tucked between his legs!

"Sinbad! Sinbad—it's *me!*" Ted exclaimed. He didn't dare to move, realizing that the dog hadn't recognized him. Had it really been that long since he'd last been home?

"Good dog, Sinbad, good watchdog!" he said more softly as the dog tilted his head to one side, peering through the darkness at the figure in front of the door. "Now smarten up, mutt—and recognize your master's voice for crying out loud!"

The growl turned to a whimper and then almost immediately to frenzied barking, as Sinbad joyfully launched himself at his "master," his large tail wagging wildly, knocking over a wicker basket filled with Christmas cards that Jillian had placed on a low table near the front door.

Obviously overcome with happiness, the animal turned himself round and round in quick circles, then deserted his usual half decently good behavior by jumping up at Ted and placing his large paws on the man's shoulders—the better to lick his master's face.

"That's better," Ted said, disengaging himself from the dog's affectionate embrace. "Wetter—but better. Now where's Jill, boy? She should have come running by now. Or am I wrong, and the only reason you're so glad to see me is because she isn't home yet and you're looking for your dinner?"

His second guess had been the right one. Jillian wasn't home and Sinbad's dish was empty.

After pouring some dry food into one dish and fresh water into the other, Ted pulled a can of iced tea from the refrigerator—noticing with a smile that the shelves seemed to be bulging with all sorts of good food, including a large ham that he decided was to be the centerpiece of the first of the Hackett "traditional" Christmas dinners—and wandered back into the dining room to press the answering-machine button labeled Memos.

There was no message from Jillian explaining her absence, but Ted took solace in the thought that she might be out buying him a last-minute present before the stores closed. With a gingerbread man stuck between his teeth, he grabbed at his luggage and headed upstairs to change out of his uniform before she got home.

He returned downstairs twenty minutes later, his hair still damp from his shower, and walked into the living room, his arms loaded with a half dozen wrapped presents he had brought with him from San Francisco.

"Well, I'll be darned," he said a few moments later, spying a box of Christmas ornaments he had forgotten he owned.

Dropping to his knees to place the presents under the tree—and resisting the urge to shake or test the weight of the presents already there—he began looking through the box. Each ornament he unearthed likewise unearthed a memory of his childhood, his parents, and the joyous Christmases they had spent together.

Carrying an ornament in the shape of a baseball with the logo of the Detroit Tigers painted on its surface, Ted headed for the kitchen as he heard Jillian's key turn in the lock.

"Slugger," he began as he entered the kitchen, "I can't tell you how wonderful it is to see these old ornaments. I didn't even remember that I still had this stuff hanging around any—*Jillian!*" He stopped dead and stared at her. "What in hell—"

"Welcome home, darling," Jillian said in greeting, smiling weakly, almost apprehensively, as Barbara hurried forward to pull out a chair and then unnecessarily ordered Jillian to sit in it.

Maneuvering herself until she was beside the chair, Jillian handed her crutches to Ted—who accepted them automatically—and then sat down, motioning toward the clear plastic "air cast" that now covered her left leg from her badly sprained ankle to just below her scraped knee.

"Look what I got for Christmas, Ted," she continued brightly, "and I didn't even have to ask Santa for it!"

Chapter Twelve

"I thought the climate would be warmer out here than it is," Jillian said as Ted adjusted the pillow beneath her sprained ankle, then leaned back against the railing of the small balcony that overlooked the street. "It can't be more than fifty degrees. Isn't this supposed to be 'sunny California'?"

Ted grinned at her. "It is sunny California, Slugger—but it's *not* Miami Beach. The California coast has more of a maritime climate, with cool summers and warm winters. Although someone told me it's a little unusual that we haven't had a frost yet."

"I didn't realize. Amazing. It's a good thing you packed for me, darling, or I'd be freezing right now instead of comfortable, even with the sun so bright.

Have I told you how much I love my new sweat suit?"

"You have," Ted answered, smiling as she stroked the sleeve of the forest green two-piece sweat suit, "but you can tell me again if you want to. I'm rather proud of the fact that I picked it out all by myself. I'm not used to buying Christmas presents for a woman. The last time I did, now that I think of it, I bought my mother a new roasting pan. Not much romance there. Are you sure you're comfortable, Slugger? I could get you another pillow if you think you need it. Tell you what—I'll get one anyway, and you can decide if you need it."

Jillian smiled up at her husband as he passed by her and back into the living room of the Mission District apartment. He'd been so wonderful, ever since the moment she had hobbled into the kitchen and presented him with a very unexpected "present"—her sprained, not broken ankle.

He had taken over the decorating of the tree, the preparation of their first annual Hackett Christmas dinner—done everything—all without a word of complaint. He hadn't even said that she would never have slipped on the ice if she lived with him in San Francisco, because there *was* no ice in San Francisco—or at least there weren't any ice *storms* in San Francisco.

And now, three days later, they were both happily ensconced in his apartment, where she would remain until the end of Baird School's Christmas break, three weeks from now. Steve was on an extended flight and wouldn't be back until it was time for him to leave for Houston on New Year's Day, so they had the place to themselves, and if her air cast was any impediment to making this interlude a second honeymoon, it was proving to be only a very small one.

And just to top it all off, Ted was waiting on her hand and foot—a circumstance she had not enjoyed since she had been ill with the flu at fifteen and her mother had been around to plump her pillows and serve up homemade chicken soup.

As she watched an older man walking his dog along the pavement, she spared a moment to think about Sinbad. She was thankful that Barbara and Pete had volunteered to take care of him. "He'll probably be spoiled rotten by the time I get home," she murmured, smiling.

"Who's going to be spoiled rotten, Slugger?" Ted asked as he reappeared on the balcony, one of the bed pillows in his hand. "I guess you mean me—at least once your ankle is healed and you take your turn as slave of all work, alphabetizing my spices—*P* comes before *S*, remember, as all I have are salt and pepper—pressing my uniforms and feeding me peeled grapes as I recline at my ease, my head in your lap."

"Is that right? You'll get your own head served to you on a silver platter if you even dare to ask me to pay you back for being a devoted husband. You're doing this out of love for your *dearest* wife, remember? Although I suppose I could press your uniforms—that is, if you ask me nicely. And you shouldn't sit there without putting down a pillow first—the floor is still damp from that rain we had earlier."

"Nag, nag, nag." Ted remained seated on the floor of the balcony, his arms wrapped around his bent knees, and grinned at her. "Gee, suddenly I'm feeling very married. But to tell you the truth, this 'in sickness and in health' thing isn't so bad. I'm glad I insisted on having you stay out here with me until you're back on your feet. Will you be cured by dinnertime, do you think? I'm getting rather bored with my own cooking."

"What cooking? *Serving* leftovers from our Christmas dinner is more like it. *Reheating* microwave breakfasts might even be better." Jillian laughed. "And here I was, thinking how wonderful you've been. So three days is your limit for the 'for better or worse' part of our vows, is it? But to tell you the truth, I'm getting rather sick of ham sandwiches and pizza myself. If I give you a list, do you think you could navigate your way through the nearest grocery store? I may be on crutches, but I can still roast a chicken. And some baked potatoes? And maybe a small salad?"

"Stop! Stop! You're killing me," Ted protested comically, scrambling to his feet while holding his stomach, as if he had been starving for the last three days. "Could you do that thing you do with fresh broccoli and cauliflower and salad dressing? I tell you, Slugger, if we could market that we could both retire to our own island in the Bahamas—it's that good."

"Flattery will get you anywhere, darling." Jillian reached behind her for her crutches, then allowed Ted to help her up. "I'll make out the list and while you're gone I'll lie on the couch, indulged, decadent female that I am, and finish the last chapter of my book."

"You've got a deal!" Ted stood back and let Jillian enter the apartment ahead of him, then grabbed a pencil and paper and jotted down everything she told him to purchase. Five minutes later, Jillian was on the couch, blissfully alone, looking through the jumble of magazines on the coffee table for her book.

She had just located it when she heard a key in the door and turned to see Steve Hammond enter, his head down as he dropped his flight bag on the floor and then kicked the door shut behind him.

"Um—hi, Steve," Jillian said, frowning in sudden apprehension. "Merry Christmas and welcome back. Ted said you wouldn't be back until New Year's Day. Is everything all right?"

"Jillian!" Steve exclaimed as he looked at her in surprise. "I didn't expect to see you." He advanced into the room and took up a seat in the chair beside the couch. "What did Ted do—kidnap you? No—

wait a minute," he continued, motioning toward her air cast. "I'll change that. Ted didn't kidnap you. He just took you dancing and then stepped all over you with his two left feet. Lord, I knew that guy would stoop to anything to get you to himself for a while—but I think maybe he outdid himself this time."

"Idiot!" Jillian laughed happily, then leaned back against the couch cushions. "Ted had nothing to do with my injury. I fell on some ice the day before Christmas. In fact, Ted has been wonderful about having to take care of me. But, Steve, answer my question, please. Is something wrong? You aren't supposed to be here—not that I'm trying to throw you out—and you look tired."

Steve exhaled his breath in a long sigh. "Exhausted is more like it. I've been awake for twenty-five—" he pushed back his sleeve and squinted at his watch "—make that twenty-*six* hours. I had just crawled into my hotel room in Honolulu when I got a telephone call telling me about my dad's heart attack and emergency open-heart surgery. Lombard's gave me an immediate compassionate leave, and I'll be on my way to Houston Intercontinental in two hours. I just stopped back here to pick up the Christmas presents I bought for the family."

Jillian sat forward and reached out a hand to touch Steve's sleeve. "I'm so sorry. How is your father?"

Steve smiled thinly. "Great," he said, shaking his head. "That man's tough as old boots. He wouldn't even let Mom tell me anything until he was off the respirator and able to speak to me himself while Mom held a phone to his ear. He was moved out of the cardiac intensive-care unit this morning—probably by the nurses themselves, who couldn't wait to be rid of him. He has to give up his cigars, you know, and he's not exactly happy about it."

Jillian relaxed, although she could still see the strain around Steve's eyes, no matter how encouraging his news about his father. "But you want to see him for yourself, don't you, Steve?" she asked, reaching for her crutches. "I don't blame you. Would you like a ham sandwich before you go? It won't be any bother—and we still have enough of it left over from our Christmas dinner to feed a small army."

"Jill, you've got yourself a deal! No wonder Ted is going to talk to the powers that be about dropping out of the program and going back to navigation. At first I thought he was nuts to give up this chance, but now I see his point. I wouldn't want to be away from a woman like you myself."

Fifteen minutes later, and still determinedly smiling, Jillian said goodbye to Steve, who had tucked two silver-foil-wrapped sandwiches in his flight bag just before he headed out the door, on his way to the airport.

She couldn't let Steve see how badly his words had shaken her. Her nerves were tied into knots. She pushed herself to slice ham and tomatoes and put together Steve's sandwiches when all she wanted to do was plunk herself down on the kitchen floor and howl like a baby.

But now Steve was gone, and Ted would be returning any moment.

There was still no time to indulge herself in a good cry, no time to carefully work out a clever way to introduce Steve's explosive information into a conversation.

There was no time for her to do anything but react, saying the first thing that came into her head as Ted, unknowing, reentered the apartment, his smile wide, his arms loaded with bulging brown-paper grocery bags. She only waited until he had slipped the chicken and other cold foods into the refrigerator before pouncing.

"You're planning to *quit?*" she accused, hating the shrillness in her voice as she propelled herself into the living room on her crutches, so that he had no choice but to follow after her. "Without telling me, without so much as a single word to me—you were going to *quit* the program—throw it all away? Ted, how *could* you?"

Ted glanced right and left, as if belatedly trying to assure himself he was in the correct apartment, then looked comprehendingly at Steve's uniform bag, which had been laid on a nearby chair. He raised one eyebrow quizzically. "I missed that when I first came in, didn't I? So, where is our coast-to-coast bigmouth?"

"Don't blame Steve—he didn't know he was telling me something you hadn't dared to do. Besides, he's gone to Houston to be with his family. His father had bypass surgery three days ago, but he's all right now. Now answer my question, Ted," Jillian demanded, lowering herself onto the couch while retaining hold of her crutches, just in case she decided it might make her feel better if she beaned Ted with one of them.

He collapsed his long frame into a nearby chair. "Steve is about a week behind in his information, Slugger. I had seriously thought of giving it all up, I admit it, and I discussed different possibilities with Steve. If I did give up my promotion, it was going to be my Christmas present to you—me showing up on Christmas Eve, with all my luggage, the *un*-conquering hero, who threw it all away for love of his woman. But I couldn't do it."

Jillian pressed a shaking hand to her mouth, feeling the sting of tears behind her eyes. "You—you couldn't?" she asked tremulously. "Why, Ted?"

He spread his hands in a helpless gesture. "I don't know. It wasn't because I don't love you, Jilly—you do know that, don't you? It would have been chickening out, I guess, if that doesn't sound too macho. We've set goals, you and I, both in our careers and for our marriage—and I almost let my loneliness for you make me forget those goals." He smiled at her. "And from your reaction just now, I'd say that in the end I made the right decision. For a minute there,

Slugger, I thought you were going to bean me with one of those crutches."

Jillian's shoulders began to shake as she chuckled softly, shaking her head. "Yeah, I know. And I also know why I overreacted. Ted—I'm already one step ahead of you. You see, I'm planning to do the same thing."

"Oh, really?" He sat forward, listening intently. "Do go on, Slugger," he urged, "I think I'm going to enjoy this."

Jillian lowered her head, intent on watching her own hands as she fiddled with one of the buttons that lined the front of her sweat suit top. "I approached Mr. Baird last week about the possibility he might give me a reference at the end of this school year—providing, of course, he allowed me out of my contract—because I have gotten about three pretty good responses to my latest job applications. It was going to be my Christmas present to you."

"Oh, it was, was it?" Ted remarked silkily, exchanging his seat on the chair for one beside Jillian on the couch. "And what did Mr. Baird say?"

Jillian sneaked a look up at Ted from beneath her lashes. "Not much. That's why it wasn't a Christmas present. He did say he'd think about it over the Christmas break, so I planned to keep everything a secret until at least the middle of January. And now, according to Steve, you almost beat me to the punch."

And then she frowned. "You know what, Ted—this is just like that old Christmas story. You remember—the one where the wife sells her hair to buy her husband a fob for his watch—"

"—and the husband sells his watch to buy his wife a comb for her hair," Ted ended, grinning. "I remember. O Henry, wasn't it?" He pulled Jillian close against his shoulder. "I thought we promised to get better about this 'communication' thing, Slugger. At the rate we're going, we'll be spending next year with you here on the coast and me in Pennsylvania."

Giggling, Jillian buried her head against Ted's chest, then lifted a hand to touch his cheek while staring up into his eyes. His beautiful, lovable, irresistible blue eyes. "I'm sorry I was so angry when you came in, darling. I think my guilty conscience got the better of me for a few minutes. That, and the fact that I also think that *I* wanted to be the one to solve all our problems."

He dropped a kiss on her forehead, then laid her back against the cushions of the couch, his hands sliding intimately along her rib cage. "Nope," he said, leaning over her. "No magic wand hidden on the lady anywhere. So—how did you plan to perform this magic trick that would solve all our problems?"

Jillian pushed him away and struggled back into a sitting position. "And who said I *haven't* solved them? If you'll remember—I still haven't heard from Mr. Baird. Anyway, if I can't make this work Barbara will probably throw me out of her wedding party. I did tell you that I'm to be her matron of honor, didn't I?"

"You did, not that I can see what Barbara's wedding plans have to do with anything," Ted concurred, still seeming to be more interested in Jillian than he was in anything she had to say on the subject of their long-distance marriage. "Have I told you how much I like your hair this way? Its shorter length makes your throat just that much more accessible to amorous exploration," he explained, then began nuzzling the sensitive skin just behind her ear. "*Yumm,* I think I just discovered new territory."

Jillian rolled her eyes in mock disapproval, then gave in momentarily to the delicious sensations caused by Ted's ministrations before forcing herself to be serious once more. "Barbara and Pete—" she began, swallowing down the impulse to leave this conversation for another time. "Barb and Pete approached me last week about buying mother's house."

Ted's hand stilled in the act of opening the row of buttons that made up the front closure of Jillian's sweat suit top. "Oh? And where does that leave us— on the street? Have you talked to Sinbad about this? I don't think our resident mutt is going to be real choked up about the idea."

Jillian snuggled closer as Ted released the last button and slid his hand inside the material, capturing her breast inside the sheer material of her bra.

"Maybe not, but it would be wonderful for Barb. She won't have to worry about her mother, because she'll be right next door, and Pete won't have to worry about her mother because she'll be all the way next door—if you get my drift."

"I'd like to drift toward the bedroom, actually," Ted responded, lowering his face to the creamy skin above Jillian's bra, "but continue. I'm listening. This almost-a-Christmas-present of yours is getting better by the minute."

Ted's meandering lips were playing havoc with Jillian's ability to keep her mind on the subject, but she took a deep breath and forced herself to go on. "School's over the second week of June, a month after the wedding, but Barb and Pete said they wouldn't mind waiting to move in until I could pack and get out. And—and Mother told me she wants to give us Barb's fifteen percent down payment as a wedding present, because I've taken such good care of the house these past years."

That caught Ted's attention and he sat up, placing his hands on Jillian's shoulders as he stared deeply into her eyes. "You're kidding," he said slowly, then added, "you're *not* kidding. Slugger—do you know what this means?"

"I've got a pretty good idea what it means, yes," she answered, "unless you say we can't accept Mom's offer because you want us to do everything on our own." This particular thought had been plaguing Jillian ever since her mother had made the offer, and now she searched Ted's face for his reaction.

He frowned slightly, bit his lip in thought and then shook his head. "Nope. I can't think of a single reason for turning your mother's offer down. It would be her gift to you, not a handout to me. You've been a great tenant, Jill—putting on a new roof, painting all the rooms, keeping the whole place in great condition. If your mother is willing, I think it's a wonderful present."

Jillian sagged against him in relief. "And you nearly handed back your promotion. I'm so sorry, Ted—I never should have kept any of this a secret. I was so tempted to tell you on Christmas Eve. You know, the single present you said we should open that night? And I probably would have, too, even if Mr. Baird hasn't quite said yes yet. But then this darn ankle got in the way, and—"

"That darn ankle, Jilly, got you to California," Ted interrupted, lifting her into his arms before heading for the bedroom, "and we're going to take advantage of that accident by spending the next two weeks looking at apartments up for rental in June. After this short detour, of course."

Jillian allowed herself to be laid down on the wide bed, then held her arms wide, silently urging her husband to join her. "Of course," she answered just before his lips met hers, "anything you want, darling—just as long as it's spontaneous."

Epilogue

Ted waved his hands in front of his face dramatically, pretending to cut through the smoke rising from the charcoal grill. "Great fire you've got going there, Pete," he said. "Hey—are those fire sirens I'm hearing?" he asked, cupping one hand around his ear.

"Don't insult the cook, darling," Jillian said as she passed by, on her way to rescue three-year-old Theodore Joseph—T.J. for short—from Barb's two-year-old terror, Pete Junior. "It's the best way I know to end up with a burned hot dog."

"That's how I like 'em," Ted called after her, smiling as he watched her go down on her knees between the two boys, explaining in her best elementary-schoolteacher tones that throwing toys at a person's head wasn't "nice." She was four months pregnant and had just begun to complain that her waistbands were getting tight, but he still thought she was the most beautiful, the sexiest woman in the world. Maybe even the universe.

"Here's the hamburgers and hot dogs, Pete," Barbara said, laying a heaping plate of uncooked meat on the picnic table. "Mother says don't burn them this year. Ted—did you have to beat poor Pete by ten strokes at golf this morning?"

"Nope," he answered, smiling at the woman who was his wife's best friend and also the world's silliest creature—if a lovable silly creature. "I could have beaten him by twelve strokes, but I took pity on him. Didn't I, Pete?"

Pete nodded and smiled, then went back to loading burgers and hot dogs onto the grill top. Ted took a sip of iced tea to cover his smile. Good old Pete. The man rarely talked, yet he seemed contented enough with his life, his wife and his son. Even with his mother-in-law.

To each his own, Ted decided. Moving away from the smoking grill, he strolled out from under the trees and into the sun, enjoying the openness of the expanse of the Lehigh Parkway they had staked out as their own for their annual Labor Day picnic. Lord knew he and Jillian hadn't exactly been a typical married couple, living the first year of their marriage out of a suitcase, until Jillian had found a teaching position in Mill Valley.

"What are you looking so smug about?" Jillian asked, coming up beside him and slipping an arm around his waist. "You may be a man of leisure right now, but don't forget that you drew the cleanup detail this year."

Ted laid an arm across Jillian's shoulders as they fell into step, walking toward the gigantic willow trees that dipped into the water of the Little Lehigh River. "I won't forget, Slugger," he said, stopping to give her a kiss. "This is nice, isn't it? The Parkway, the kids, the comfortable predictability. Another Labor Day, another picnic, another burned hamburger. I'm glad we decided to come back. California's great, but we've got roots here."

"Roots," Jillian agreed quickly, "one-and-one-half kids, an overgrown dog who has a thing for digging in my flower beds, a lovely home and a hefty mortgage. I can't imagine anything more married than that. Oh yes—and a station wagon. Every suburban couple needs a station wagon. It's hard to believe we ever lived a continent away from each other."

Ted felt something tugging at his leg, stopped, and glanced down to see that T.J. had come to join them. The child wrapped his arms around his father's knee as he tried to place both sneakered feet on one of Ted's larger feet, so that when Ted took a step, T.J. moved along right with it.

"Keep walking, Daddy," T.J. prodded, grinning up at him. "I'll hold on."

Ted smiled back at his son, seeing a miniature reflection of his wife in the boy's eyes and in his mop of dark, coppery hair, then looked at Jillian, loving her with all his heart. "We sure will hold on, won't we, Slugger?" he said, taking a step forward, out of the shade of the towering oak trees, and into the sun. "We're Hacketts—and it's what we do best."

* * * * *

Is your father a Fabulous Father?

Then enter him in Silhouette Romance's

"FATHER OF THE YEAR" Contest
and you can both win some great prizes! Look for contest details in the FABULOUS FATHER titles available in June, July and August...

ONE MAN'S VOW by Diana Whitney
Available in June

ACCIDENTAL DAD by Anne Peters
Available in July

INSTANT FATHER by Lucy Gordon
Available in August

Only from

Silhouette
R O M A N C E™

SRFD

Take 4 bestselling love stories FREE

Plus get a FREE surprise gift!

Special Limited-time Offer

Mail to Silhouette Reader Service™

    3010 Walden Avenue
    P.O. Box 1867
    Buffalo, N.Y. 14269-1867

YES! Please send me 4 free Silhouette Romance™ novels and my free surprise gift. Then send me 6 brand-new novels every month, which I will receive months before they appear in bookstores. Bill me at the low price of $1.99* each plus 25¢ delivery and applicable sales tax, if any.* That's the complete price and—compared to the cover prices of $2.75 each—quite a bargain! I understand that accepting the books and gift places me under no obligation ever to buy any books. I can always return a shipment and cancel at any time. Even if I never buy another book from Silhouette, the 4 free books and the surprise gift are mine to keep forever.

215 BPA AJH5

Name _____ (PLEASE PRINT) _____

Address _____ Apt. No. _____

City _____ State _____ Zip _____

This offer is limited to one order per household and not valid to present Silhouette Romance™ subscribers.
*Terms and prices are subject to change without notice. Sales tax applicable in N.Y.

USROM-93R   ©1990 Harlequin Enterprises Limited

Silhouette Books
is proud to present
our best authors,
their best books...
and the best in
your reading pleasure!

Throughout 1993, look for exciting
books by these top names in
contemporary romance:

DIANA PALMER—
Fire and Ice in June

ELIZABETH LOWELL—
Fever in July

CATHERINE COULTER—
Afterglow in August

LINDA HOWARD—
Come Lie With Me in September

When it comes to passion,
we wrote the book.

BOBT2

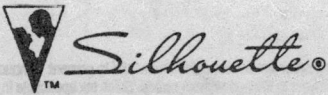

HE'S MORE THAN A MAN, HE'S ONE OF OUR

INSTANT FATHER
Lucy Gordon

Gavin Hunter had always dreamed that his son, Peter, would follow in his footsteps. Then his wife left him, taking their child with her. When fate reunited father and son six years later, they were strangers. And with the boy's mother dead, Gavin blamed the child's guardian, Norah Ackroyd. But soon Gavin found loving Norah was easier than blaming her.

Share Gavin's triumph as he wins the heart of his young son and the love of a good woman in Lucy Gordon's INSTANT FATHER, available in August.

Fall in love with our **Fabulous Fathers** and join the Silhouette Romance family!

FF893

Fifty red-blooded, white-hot, true-blue hunks from every State in the Union!

Beginning in May, look for MEN MADE IN AMERICA! Written by some of our most popular authors, these stories feature fifty of the strongest, sexiest men, each from a different state in the union!

Two titles available every other month at your favorite retail outlet.

In July, look for:

CALL IT DESTINY by Jayne Ann Krentz (Arizona)
ANOTHER KIND OF LOVE by Mary Lynn Baxter (Arkansas)

In September, look for:

DECEPTIONS by Annette Broadrick (California)
STORMWALKER by Dallas Schulze (Colorado)

You won't be able to resist MEN MADE IN AMERICA!

If you missed your state or would like to order any other states that have already been published, send your name, address, zip or postal code, along with a check or money order (please do not send cash) for $3.59 for each book, plus 75¢ postage and handling ($1.00 in Canada), payable to Harlequin Reader Service, to:

In the U.S.
3010 Walden Avenue
P.O. Box 1369
Buffalo, NY 14269-1369

In Canada
P.O. Box 609
Fort Erie, Ontario
L2A 5X3

Please specify book title(s) with order.
Canadian residents add applicable federal and provincial taxes.

MEN793

SMYTHESHIRE, MASSACHUSETTS.

Small town. Big secrets.

Silhouette Romance invites you to visit Elizabeth August's intriguing small town, a place with an unusual legacy rooted deep in the past....

THE VIRGIN WIFE (#921) February 1993
HAUNTED HUSBAND (#922) March 1993
LUCKY PENNY (#945) June 1993
A WEDDING FOR EMILY (#953) August 1993

Elizabeth August's SMYTHESHIRE, MASSACHUSETTS—
This sleepy little town has plenty to keep you up at night.
Only from Silhouette Romance!

If you missed any of the SMYTHESHIRE, MASSACHUSETTS titles, *The Virgin Wife* (SR #921, $2.69), *Haunted Husband* (SR #922, $2.69) or *Lucky Penny* (SR #945, $2.75), order your copy now by sending your name, address, zip or postal code, along with a check or money order (please do not send cash) for the amount listed above, plus 75¢ postage and handling ($1.00 in Canada), payable to Silhouette Books, to:

In the U.S.

Silhouette Books
3010 Walden Avenue
P.O. Box 1396
Buffalo, NY 14269-1396

In Canada

Silhouette Books
P.O. Box 609
Fort Erie, Ontario
L2A 5X3

Please specify book title(s) with your order.
Canadian residents add applicable federal and provincial taxes.

SREA-4